David Nabhan

The Pilots of Borealis

To my family,
and to my friends and colleagues on the West Coast

Cover Illustration by Mihailo Vukelic
"Borealis"

ISBN-13 978-1463777968
ISBN-10 1463777965
BISAC: Fiction/Science Fiction/General

RED LION PUBLISHING

Other works by David Nabhan:
Forecasting the Catastrophe (2010)
Predicting the Next Great Quake (1996)
Visit our website: www.earthquakepredictors.com
davidwrites200@aol.com

Printed in the USA

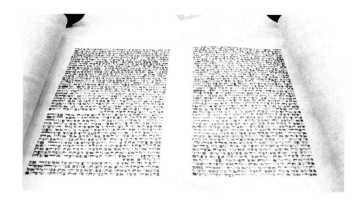

Every gun that is made, every warship launched, every rocket fired signifies a theft from those who hunger and are not fed, from those who are cold and are not clothed. But not just money is spent for arms. The sweat of laborers, the genius of scientists, and the hopes of children are wasted too. This is not a way of life in any true sense. Under the cloud of war, it is humanity hanged on an iron cross.

Dwight D. Eisenhower, April 16, 1953

Chapter One

Rumors of War

The few citizens of Borealis not out on the terraces looking up to the Epsilon Observation Deck were those in Sick Bay, and a number of them had struggled to their feet to witness the event too. The crowds and activity seemed to buoy up the old adage that Borealis never slept. Most thought that was due to the case that night didn't exist here. It was a common misunderstanding since it was a select group of human beings, indeed, who'd ever seen the place with their own eyes. The constant, lively bustle was more grounded in the fact that there had always been something to do since Settlement Times, and that industrious habit was instilled in every Borelian from childhood. Few things could bring the city to a standstill, except maybe a good piloting match—Borelians were absolute fanatics for piloting. And this one was going to be a good one. The media thought so too. The match was being beamed out to the five billion people living on the Terran Ring and also to the quarter trillion people in every Alliance below on Earth. The pundits of the innumerable news services had run like crazy with the build-up, dissecting for their audiences every byzantine twist to the story. This was more than just a possible monument in human endurance and grace, they explained. For Nerissa was flying for Borealis, and Borealis' cause, in front of her fellow citizens, under Borealis' Dome.

Demetrius Sehene, her arch-rival from the Terran Ring, didn't come a quarter million miles to lose either though. There was a dark horse, too, and the commentators hadn't ignored this angle either. Quite a number of them were asking aloud what was to be made of Clinton Rittener in this contest. None of the analysts could seem to have imagined that the next time he'd surface would be in a *piloting* match. More stunning for everyone in the Inner Solar System was that Clinton Rittener was actually showing his face in such a public way, and more shocking, so close to Earth and the Terran Ring. Neither was ever out of sight for anyone willing to exit the Dome and climb the escarpments that ringed the city. The view of the Terran Ring from the Moon, hanging around Earth like a metallic halo, was the most iconic image of the day. Everyone who saw it lost their breath.

The more sage commentators explained that Borealis was the only place in which a man like Clinton Rittener *could* show his face. Certainly, he was a hero to billions of people on Earth but it was doubted that anyone alive had also made as many enemies, and of the kind who'd find no expedient too nasty for them to eschew if it meant they could get their hands on him. Some were wondering aloud why the Council even allowed him to compete, so sure were they that an assassination attempt was at least being planned.

Nerissa, like everyone else on the Moon, was known only by her given name. Borelians had long since dispensed with the use of last names, a source of but one of many differences between themselves and the Terrans living in the stupendous, planet-girdling megalopolis orbiting Earth. Borelians considered their amazingly few—yet obviously elite—numbers small enough that surnames were superfluous. There weren't even a quarter of a million people living on the Moon and any new arrival or newborn simply chose another name not already listed on the Citizen Roll. Borelians didn't need to say out loud what that said about their opinions about themselves, nor was it required. Their arrogant pride and outrageous stubbornness was one of the few things upon which the people of Earth and the Terran Ring could both agree. The Borelians got under everyone's skin. Yet tens of billions of pairs of eyes were nonetheless glued to the event, internally torn between having to betray their addiction to something so totally Borelian, and yet hoping that they might witness Nerissa and her haughty supporters going down in flames.

Actually, quite a few were saying that this might be the last great piloting event for a while, leaving unsaid what that meant, and allowing the words to sink in as a plainly spoken threat to the overbearing Borelians. The pessimists had reason lately to mutter such bellicose warnings as actual shooting incidents had been taking place with worrisome regularity. Squadrons of ships from both sides had been brushing wingtips in the space between the Ring and the Moon, feint being met with counter-feint. Only a week before the entire population of Borealis had rushed into the safety of the Core, and done so with astounding quickness, sealing the locks with everyone but a few stragglers inside within the amazing time of one minute and fifty-two seconds. The authorities never explained what had happened to precipitate the event, and no one outside of Borealis even knew that such a drastic defensive move had even taken place, much less how long it took. Nor was the Council on Borealis willing to allow the news off the Moon; anyone who even spoke of it could be deemed a traitor and risk extremely grave consequences. There *were* though nervous whispers exchanged in private between apprehensive citizens who quite naturally had to wonder if the system of impenetrable shields protecting the city was everything it was touted to be. Privately, even the mad scramble that had emptied their city within the cone of lunar regolith upon which the colony was built, even this astounding evacuation in less than two minutes had many on the Council worried. Borealis might not have two minutes in the worst case scenarios they were examining, but that was of a nature so classified that no level high enough existed as the proper repository for such secrets.

In any event, to the amazement of almost every soul in the Solar System, it had been decided that the match would nonetheless be held. The pretense that normalcy prevailed fooled no one, when everyone knew that "normal" was the last thing one might say about where relations between the Terran Ring, Earth and Borealis stood.

The recent scare had laid bare to the Borelians themselves just how serious the State was to protect itself, and how far it would go. Almost every doctor and nurse in the newer, exterior sick bays, for example, had immediately rushed into the Core the moment the alarm sounded and left those who couldn't move right where they lay in bed. In the one instance where medical staff disobeyed orders and wasted precious time trying to move the infirm, internal locks were employed, sealing off from the inside those compartments and leaving the scofflaws in that section of the city to whatever fate was in store. Arrests had been threatened within hours of the "all clear" and the Council was determined that nothing like it should happen again.

Every patient on Borealis was now crowded into the ancient and original Sick Bay within the Core; it was going to be that way for a while.

Even the most rabid Terran who ascribed nothing but the worst to Borealis' interests couldn't appreciate how deeply and gravely the Borelians had moved to the idea that war was sooner or later inevitable. The only questions for the Council were how to delay the conflict until the opportune moment, and how to handle the "Earth torries" in their midst when push must come to shove. Earth, that unintelligible, incoherent, confused patchwork of ephemeral Alliances that came and went with the seasons, could be counted on to do just the opposite of what seemed to be in its own interests, never mind Borealis' benefit. And yet love of the mother planet was alive here still after so many centuries, albeit the kind of logic-defying love that binds parent with child, even as one of them descends into the insane self-destruction in which Earth had dwelt for generations now. Every single word, every smile and frown, every unrestrained grimace or cheer during the coming contest was to be monitored and recorded, according to the rumors, and hopefully a complete catalogue of the citizens rooting for Rittener, Earth's antihero, would emerge. This, said those supposedly in the know, was the real motive for the Council's decision not to cancel the piloting match.

Everyone in the Inner Solar System, from as far out as the lawless mining outposts in the Asteroid Belt and the dusty Martian colonies, and back to Earth again would be watching—and wondering about an impending war. The Borelian Council appeared willing to take on the immense power of the Terran Ring, seemed determined to free itself from its influence, and inaugurate a *truly* independent

Borealis. After years of debate it had come to that. When the Terrans made their next heavy-handed move, which the Council could certainly count on, Borealis might finally be ready to meet force with force. It seemed interested only in steering the final feints and thrusts in such a way that history should mark the Terrans as the aggressors. The events of the last week showed that the Terrans were much of the same mind. If millions or billions were to die in the impending struggle, each side wished the onus to be upon the other.

When Nerissa emerged onto the Observation Deck an immediate roar from tens of thousands of Borelians went up, a cry so load and powerful that it seemed to reverberate off the dome that encased the city. She was helped to strap on her oversize and unwieldy wings, and then stepped onto her launch pad and gave the citizens her hallmark pose, with her wings outstretched and her face fixed with the iconic, aloof look of Borelian superiority. No one in the Solar System could mistake her; she looked like no other flyer in history. She certainly seemed almost totally nude—barefoot and wearing nothing save the skimpiest, most diaphanous lycraplastique brief and top; it was said to weigh less than a lunar gram. Her hair was as thick and black as the image of the Roman goddess of the Moon, Diana, on Borealis' Great Seal. It was tightly twisted into an ebony braid that fell almost to the small of her back. As she stood on her podium displaying her wingspan, every contour of her impossibly muscled body strained for the audience of over five hundred billion. As stunning as she was—malachite green eyes, chiseled patrician face, perfect pert breasts upturned by taut muscles that rippled from her lower abdomen to her rib cage—even the most lascivious would be struck first with

15

just a plain and unavoidable admiration for the classic beauty of her ultra-perfect feminine form. Journalists had long since ceased to ask if she felt ashamed to fly so scantily clad.

"We have a different view of the human body," she had so often curtly answered in the past, "much different than the pornography-addicted degeneracy of the Terran Ring."

This was an historic insult that was meant to sting. One of the pistons that powered the development of the Terran Ring was the economics of sex in its first century. The sex tourist industry, which offered the never before experienced allure of coitus in weightlessness, was in fact just a footnote in history. Borelians, however, never allowed an opportunity to pass without reminding Terrans about it.

She could have been mistaken for a statue, standing so erect and motionless at the highest point above the city, her skin the same rich color of flawless beige alabaster, like smooth wheat porcelain. Such a complexion was certainly far from unusual for many residents of the lunar colony, for Borealis had been built almost precisely on the Moon's North Pole, quite near to the immense stores of ice which had lain frozen for eons at the bottom of deep craters, in perpetual shadow and cold. The city itself never saw the *direct* Sun, for it too had been built around a thick cone of lunar regolith, thrusting up from the floor of a perfectly situated crater and surrounded on all sides by natural sun shields. Reflected light though, incessant but mild, bathed the city unremittingly, and gave Borelian women a beautiful skin texture and tone found only here. The "dayglow" gave life to everything on Borealis and suffused its women with a healthy yet seductive beauty. That, and the feeble lunar gravity that permitted limbs much longer, more lithe and lissome than on weighty Earth, made Borelian women into tall, supple greyhounds. And Nerissa, the image of Borelian beauty, didn't have a gram of weight in the wrong place. Visitors walking the streets of Borealis were taken aback by the fact that not a single overweight citizen was to be seen, the entire population having long since put food and carnal desires far down the list of their priorities. And, although it wasn't actually against the law to eat meat, no one could remember the last time anyone had done it. It was considered a thoroughly disgusting habit, a hallmark of the aboriginal culture that had been thankfully left behind for the "cannibal" hoi poloi on fetid Earth, or of the sensate "gluttons" on the Terran Ring.

Clinton Rittener was on the pad next to her, and he'd told himself this luck of the draw meant nothing and that he wasn't going to give her a first, much less second look. He simply couldn't restrain himself though. And with her being so close, the glances hadn't any hope but becoming stares. The dayglow on her body revealed just the slightest girlish freckling on her slender form, and cast alluring shadows on the curves that were nonetheless quite real, supple sensual curves that hadn't been erased. No one trained like Nerissa, yet no matter how desperately the Spartan regimen had striven to beat the iron in her into steel, she was nonetheless still not only quite female, but a most strikingly beautiful woman. In a moment of weakness he turned to her and spoke.

"I'd like to wish you…" That's all he got out. She turned so quickly and fixed him with such a cold, deadly stare that the "good luck" caught in his throat. It stunned him, stealing his words and leaving him with just the look they were sharing, she also refusing to take her eyes off him. He could see now that her hair had raven tufts and faint streaks running through it; it wasn't as jet black as he had first thought. The subtle color complimented the blood-red lips and pink nipples pressing through the tissue-thin halter. She arched her eyebrows as she calmly spoke, a firm composure that stoically restrained what quite honestly could almost seem to be identified as a roiling hatred.

"You're Clinton…Rittener, aren't you?" She paused between names, letting him know in no uncertain terms what disdain she felt for a supposed Borelian who sported an Earth name. She shook her head slightly as if wondering to herself under what confused cloud this man must live. She didn't wait for a response.

"What are you *doing* here, anyway?" she blurted out. She nodded at the throngs who now stood silently watching the encounter. "You're not part of us. Why *are* you even here?" She sniffed her delicate nose up at him in a way that told him she smelled grease on him, and was revolted by it.

"So what sort of game are you playing, Clinton…Rittener?"

Clinton Rittener had been accused of many things in his forty-two years, but playing games had never been one of the charges. In fact, in this new age of a quarter of a trillion humans crowding out any opportunity for individual accomplishment, he was considered far and wide to be perhaps one of humanity's last best chances for personal heroism. The list of men respected on Earth and admired also in Borealis was a very, very short one. The Borelians didn't hand out honorary citizenship to just anyone; in fact, the last time it had happened was more than a decade ago. There had been almost unanimous support for it, but that was before all the saber-rattling. And many, like Nerissa, would obviously be pleased to see it revoked. That wouldn't be easy though, for in all the Inner Solar System, there was just one Clinton Rittener.

Chapter Two

In the Service of the Terran Ring

Clinton Rittener's Danish father was the European Union's ambassador to the Asian Alliance, his mother an English heiress whose dowry came in money so old its provenance was difficult indeed to identify, but at least going back to the early 21st century. He might have grown up fat, spoiled and lazy, but even as a child he seemed marked for greatness. His aptitude for mathematics and languages was both stunning and inexplicable, for it was said that he never spoke a word for the first three years of his life. He made up for that later with more than a dozen languages both Eastern and Western, and spoken with such fluency that he could play native in more than a few of them. He had mastered trigonometry by the age of ten, calculus by twelve, and had set the Earth's scientific academies on their heels when he published a proof of Galean's Eigenvector Conjecture— which ran in the peer-reviewed journal *Aegis*…on his twenty-first birthday! It took a battery of nanocomputers several weeks to find the errors in his proof, but the sword had been drawn from the scabbard nonetheless, and it was plain to see that the blade was sharp indeed.

No one could have guessed, though, what fate had in store for Clinton Rittener. The whole world was taken by surprise when the Fifth Planetary Depression let loose Armageddon. Ten million people were killed in Shanghai alone in the opening days, along with both his parents, when mobs stormed the embassy. He was dragged half-dead from his previously cosseted world into the hinterlands of China by a faction loyal to the European Union, and there spent the next six years of his life fighting in the horrific Great Eastern War. He never spoke a single word of it—to anyone, ever—after the armistice. But it is certain that the pyramids of severed heads, the thousands of miles of crucified bodies that lined Asia's roads, and other unspeakable atrocities, changed him forever. The stories they tell about his cruelty and brutality are hard to verify and almost certainly exaggerated. It is true, though, that he most certainly was as ruthless and cold-hearted as any of the soldiers in that planet-wide bloodbath. Both the Asian Alliance and the European Union offered him high military commissions when the war ended. He declined, took the remnants of his lost inheritance, and bought passage when the first maglev up the slopes of Kilamanjaro became operational again, into orbit and onto the Terran Ring, and then straight off for Mars. He never set foot on Earth again.

About the next years spent on Mars, with forays into the depths of the Outer Solar System, not much is known except for one thing for sure: Rittener learned how to fly on Mars. Mars still is a fairly wild place, and the perfect locale to lose oneself in the "Underground," in every sense. Anything goes on Mars, and most of it is going on under the surface, including piloting. Everything though has that certain Martian twist and the sport is no exception. It's so much harder to fly on Mars that it's a good thing it's done inside kilometer-long corridors that slope gradually down into the planet's surface. Pilots get pulled down by gravity a little more than twice as strong as Luna's, so it's just as well that Martian pilots fly inside and not from cliffs. Piloting on the Red Planet is therefore devoid of maneuver, but Martian pilots are some of the most physically chiseled athletes in existence. Having trained on Mars, piloting in contests on the Moon makes them serious contenders because of their stamina advantage. Rittener joined a select corps of crack former soldiers at this strategic borderline between the Inner and Outer Solar System, many of them amateur pilots. These men—part tactician, stateless warlord, and émigré *condottierio*—formed an elite pool of mercenaries. A shadowy zeitgeist played out below ground on Mars, as assassins, spies, pirates and agents attracted from everywhere, toward every purpose, were drawn to this free-wheeling, subterranean gloom land. One of their number, Clinton Rittener, was enlisted by the Terran Archonate itself, when the miners on the Asteroid Belt revolted.

The Terran Ring had more or less sat out the recent planet-wide war, happy to see their economic and military rivals below annihilate themselves. Earth would, of course, never be the same again. Most historians were already marking this as the great turning point, the watershed when the Terran Ring in quick, successive stages became the cultural and political seat of humankind. Earth, having finally pushed her powers of recuperation past the reserve, degenerated into an insatiable market and a limitless labor pool lying beneath Terra, a supine, fallen colossus. When Clinton arrived the great renaissance was already dawning and there would have been a hundred positions open to a man like him. He hardly unpacked though, accepting a quasi-military commission offered to him by the highest body on Terra, the Archonate, to put down an insurrection that had echoed from the conflagration that had brought Mother Earth so low.

The Terrans saw their moment in the Sun dawn and they were determined to take advantage of it. For one thing, all the mineral wealth the Asteroid Belt exported to the Inner Solar System would transit through the Terran Ring. That is to say, the staggering output of iron, nickel, copper, aluminum, magnesium, gold, silver and all the rest—all of it—would be bought exclusively by the Terran Ring. The miners on the Asteroid Belt need not concern themselves with their prior contracts with war-weary, undependable consortiums on Earth, for those instruments were declared null and void, by the Terrans. Earth needed some time to catch its breath. With the mother planet in a state of near-chaos and a sizeable fraction of its population swept away, the Terran Ring's enforced stewardship was seen as a kindness—by the Terrans themselves, of course. The Terrans would see to deliveries of those metals to Earth, or anywhere else in their new "sphere of influence," as was deemed necessary. All the miners of the Belt needed to know was that the final destination for their goods was Terra. There was just one other point too: the price had fallen…dramatically. Terra would pay roughly half the pre-war price.

At first the miners just laughed, joking that maybe a new strain of venereal disease was playing havoc with the Terrans' faculties. When they realized that the Terran Ring meant business, outrage set in. Depending on whose envoy were speaking and in which interplanetary forum, there was quite a divergence of opinion about what sort of control

24

Terra legally had over the Asteroid Belt. Several attempts at negotiation broke down, and in the end the miners stubbornly just walked away; in Terra's eyes turning to open rebellion.

It would be a very nasty business to wage a war on the frontiers of the solar system in the vacuum of space, against the sparse settlements that clung to city-sized blocks of metal and rock that meandered between Mars and Jupiter. Beyond that it would no doubt be viewed as immoral and illegal by Terra's rivals. Worse still, though, would be the severe withdrawal pain that Terra was desperate to avoid should the unending transports of ore cease to arrive. Dozens of settlements in the Belt were either threatening or had already enacted embargo. While neither side was going to find this pleasant in the least, Terra only focused on ending it. What the Ring was looking for was a quick *fait accompli* that could be presented to everyone, and one that gave them the option of plausible deniability if they needed it—or implausible even. They had just the man for this job. Tactics were purposely left broadly and vaguely described. Those that wouldn't knuckle under "should be militarily convinced." Not many had any real idea what was happening half a billion miles from Earth out past Mars. If a few scruffy, unwashed, misanthropes living on the edge of existence in the dead of space were to disappear, well, had they ever really even been there, in the first place? Miners on the Asteroid Belt were as difficult to make out as shadows on Pluto. Clinton Rittener was given his privateering marque, duly signed and sealed, and told to bring them around, move them off, or wipe them out—whichever were easiest.

And here is where he made his name.

25

The *Peerless* was well-named. She was fast, reliable, and armed to the teeth. The ship was a hybrid-class destroyer, built to patrol the space between Earth and the Jovian System. No one knew what kind of swath she cut in the solar wind, but according to rumors that leaked in from listening posts at the far edges of the Solar System, her Quarrie superconducting ports sucked in so much of the solar wind that she cast a shadow as far out as the moons of Saturn. The fact that she was engineered without even a thought to artificial gravity meant that she was intended to be constantly accelerating, and fast. But if her journey from Terran orbit out to the Asteroid Belt was to be a quick one, once there she kicked into another gear. Her fusion reactor, fed by helium-3 from Borealis, was capable of ingesting and spitting out absolutely anything. She fed on the detritus she was meant to patrol, ejecting stupendous quantities of ionized flotsam that had been broiled down to pure nucleonic matter. In theory, once within the confines of the Belt, there was no limit to her speed or her range. The same reactor powered her armament and defenses; both were terrifying. *Peerless* would be an incredibly hard gnat to swat, as she was impervious to laser and particle beam salvos, in the short-run anyway.

She could go anywhere she pleased, at speeds and ranges that were quite impressive, fairly immune from attack unless by multiple opponents, and with the offensive power to erase planetoids from existence. Peerless was armed with twin punches: a high-powered electron laser capable of melting through twelve inches of steel in less than a second, and a particle beam accelerator that emitted tremendous bursts of protons at just under the speed of light. The beam pulses could shred mountain-sized chunks of pure titanium. Little wonder that the Terran Ring sent only one ship, under one captain, to bring the miners on Valerian-3 to heel. It was not only all that was required—it was overkill.

The *Peerless* slipped out of Earth orbit riding the inertia of the half-kilometer long steam piston that catapulted the ship from the Tycho Brahe Bay. The Moon was new, on the other side of Earth, so Borealis might literally have been in the dark concerning its departure. As far as Terra was concerned *any* glimmer of light shed on this operation would be too much. The mission was under the highest secrecy protocols. Rittener, seated in the captain's swivel, noted the comforting green streaks across the virtual console of the *Peerless*.

"Valid indications across the board, First Officer," Rittener said in a monotone. Lieutenant Andrews responded in the same flat timbre.

"Valid indications, roger," he said.

The ship's fusion reactor was up and running.

"Engineering?" Rittener called out in shorthand.

"All in, Captain. Ready to initiate spars on your mark," Ensign Gutierrez answered.

Peerless' spars unfurled, splaying open like a giant umbrella around the axis of the ship itself. Within an hour the superconducting segments, kept frigid by the vacuum of space, had telescoped out to form kilometer long spokes radiating out from *Peerless*. The enormous electric flux pumped through them from the ships reactor created a magnetic sail that extended much, much farther out, bouncing back a wide enough swath of the million mile an hour flood of alpha particles in the solar wind to constantly accelerate the ship to close to half a g. Duty on the ceaselessly accelerating *Peerless* felt a lot like standing still on Mars. If the rare glitch were to have occurred, things would have gone awry by now, so Rittener confidently put the ship's system on autopilot.

"Helmsman, the course is to Valerian-3." It was one of the few, laconic phrases Rittener had uttered to anyone since the crew had come aboard. "Max speed."

Lt. Andrews had certainly noticed Rittener's reluctance to waste words and he responded with nothing more than requisite.

"Roger, Valerian-3, max speed."

The *Peerless* nimbly darted toward the black ink of space, her acceleration bringing the blessed feeling of artificial gravity. The crew could finally sink into their chairs and feel the comforting reassurance of their own weight, albeit Martian weight. Rittener now addressed the ship'second officer as he rose and exited the bridge.

"Ensign Gutierrez, I'll have a word with the entire crew in the contingency galley, at the top of the hour. All hands."

"Aye, Captain. As ordered," she answered. Her Spanish accent was thick.

There was nothing perfunctory about Rittener's address to his assembled crew, it was all pure business.

"I'm going to dispense with the 'welcome aboard' speech. I'm sure every crewman has a pretty good idea of what this mission is about. There's not much more really I need add. We've been tasked with the mission to bring the mining settlements on the Asteroid Belt into compliance with an executive order of the Archonate itself, and that's exactly what we're going to do. They've suspended all shipments of vital materials and have given every indication that they haven't the slightest interest in further negotiation. It's going to be our job to change their minds and get those shipments flowing again."

Rittener paused a moment, surveying his crew. The eye contact told him something wasn't quite right but it was nothing more than just an inkling.

"Our first destination is Valerian-3. It's not the biggest of the settlements but it exports quite respectable quantities of manganese and titanium."

Again he gave each crew member a hard look. He couldn't discern a flicker of anything coming back.

"Also, Valerian-3, according to reports, can be considered one of the ringleaders of this rebellion. With all of us pulling together and a bit of luck, this might be over in short order." Rittener slowly leaned back, put a finger to the corner of his mouth and waited for comments. When he realized they weren't coming he asked.

"Questions?"

Ensign Araceli Gutierrez had one. "Well, sir, are we just showing the flag, or what?"

Rittener, of course, didn't like the question. "Come again, Ensign?"

Gutierrez would have been one of the very last souls of the five billion on the Terran Ring to come away with an award for naivety. One look into her coal black eyes is all it usually took for people to realize what a strong personality dwelt behind them. She spoke plainly, never parsing her words. Rittener had reviewed her file, what there was of it anyway. She'd joined the Service at the first opportunity, just a few days after her eighteenth birthday. Gutierrez hadn't opted for the officers' corps though. It hadn't taken long however for her superiors to recognize that she possessed potential talent for operations of the nanocryptology at the heart of much of the ship's vital systems. She was given a commission in her mid-twenties, having spent her entire career so far on the Terran Ring itself. Her closest friends called her "Chilanga" since she was born in what had been the Mexico City State, but Gutierrez left Earth with her family for the Ring when she was in pigtails. It was her great plan to save enough credits to go back and visit her birthplace; of course, that plan was off the table now. One could still see the black smudge from space, from the observation decks of the Terran Ring, the cauterized wound that had been at one time the capital of the Spanish-speaking universe. She was almost cashiered when she overheard a colleague ask jokingly how many *chilangos* could fit into a maglev shuttle. When he gave out the punch line of a hundred million, in just the dust collectors alone, he wound up in sick bay and she in the Service brig. None of that either was in the file Rittener perused, although he did wonder how such a gifted cadet could have languished at the junior officer level for so long. She was pushing thirty, even though she wouldn't have looked the least bit silly in pigtails, even now.

"Come again, Ensign?" He wasn't picturing her in pigtails now. She reminded him too much of the black-haired beauties he'd fought with in China. A few of their faces passed through his mind as he fixed his eyes on her. He'd seen so many of them with a fire burning in them that no power in the Solar System could extinguish, a fire they took courageously to their deaths, one after the other, without so much as a whimper when the end came. She

30

seemed to have the same kind of cinders smoldering inside her too.

"Permission to speak candidly, Sir?" That question never preceded anything good and Rittener would just have soon declined. He pretended that he was pleased by it nonetheless.

"Of course, Ensign. By all means, speak your mind."

"Well, we *must* be just showing the flag." She gestured with a self-explanatory and yet almost exasperated wave of her hand. "There are *twelve* of us. How are we supposed to enforce the orders of the Archonate? This is one hell of an occupation force for an entire Asteroid Belt. Do you think they sent too many of us, Captain?"

Berti Werth and Nicholas Yushenko, both inseparable, both hardly indistinguishable, both let out barely restrained snickers.

The last decades had passed without either Werth or Yushenko taking much notice; here were two "Tartars" in the flesh, but who were yet born long after the time that the fad had started to fade. Their perfectly spherical and thick-boned skulls were shaven, save for tufts of straight, blonde hair left growing at the crown and braided to the nape of the neck. On closer inspection, the style didn't fit Werth so well; his happy, round German face was simply too amicable. He looked like a Viking that you just might be able to befriend over a stein of mead. They had the Tartar mantra, "a thousand before I die," tattooed across the jugular in red and black Old Mongolian script. This duo gave the impression of the type that drank mare's blood and decorated their quarters in the faux-yert style, as if out on the wilds of the Eurasian steppes. No self-respecting Borelian would have even breathed the same air in their vicinity, for they

31

were walking, talking advertisements of everything that was loathed about Terrans and their Ring. Both were huge, strapping horses of men. Werth measured in at 6' 5", 265 standard Earth pounds; on the Ring, of course, he tipped the scales at 286 Terran pounds. The Russian was a bit shorter and a few pounds lighter but that somehow made him appear the more intimidating of the two. The pair had obviously spent a good fraction of their lives in the gymnasium and their bodies broadcast that fact. Werth would have little trouble killing the average human being with his bare hands. Yushenko, though, the more evil-looking doppeleganger, looked like he could do it quicker, much like a sleek panther. His pale blue eyes seemed to say he'd enjoy it more than Werth, too. Taking in the measure of these two Rittener wondered how the Terran Ring had managed the sagacity to escape being dragged into the incalculable, planet-wide cataclysm that had ravaged Earth. There were tens of millions of Werths and Yushenkos on the Ring.

"Seaman 2nd Class Yushenko, tell me something," Rittener asked matter-of-factly. Yushenko thought he was about to receive a dressing down for his lack of respect, but he thought wrong. "You're obviously in pretty good shape. I guess what they say about the artificial gravity on the Ring is true after all, huh?"

It was a fact. You could definitely feel the difference on the Ring—1.08 g's. New arrivals from Earth took a little time to get used to it. Of course, the slight, nagging malaise that it produced in the native-born on Earth was a crushing weight for Borelians. They were accustomed to one sixth Earth's gravity. Lunar diplomats, businessmen, and other visitors had to be quartered in those "higher" sections of the

Ring which mimicked perfectly the Moon's gravity and in which Terran pilots trained. Since the gravity on Terra was artificial, it weakened progressively the further "up" one ventured from the deck. As pilots' strength invariably gave out and as they sank lower to the "ground" floors, the stronger the force of artificial gravity became. So Terran pilots could fly almost interminably in the loftiest concentric layers of the Ring but the mettle of flyers was tested as pilots dared to fly lower and lower.

"It's simple physics, skipper," Yushenko answered in perfect New English. "It's all inertia. Once you get something spinning, well, that's the hard part. After that it's all downhill and you can coast."

He smiled broadly now, happy to have shed some light on this aspect of Terran civilization for his foreign commander. Rittener could see his muscles flex, the rippling effect obvious under the military tunic that barely contained his formidable torso.

"But, you're right. You can't get ramjets like these any place other than Terra." He glanced down at his bulging biceps to make sure Rittener understood his slang.

The Terran Ring produced the best human specimens anywhere. The Terrans were sure of it; their history and culture buoyed up that opinion too. First, they had the gravitational edge, their bodies from birth being constrained to train to bear the additional burden. And in the early days before the dozens of sky hooks made access to the Ring as simple as an elevator ride—albeit a *long* one—the scarcest commodity on the Ring were the people required to man this amazing habitat. It grew faster than people could fill it and the State took draconian measures to make up the shortfall. Terran law, cobbled together over those first centuries, when hard utilitarian decisions were the only shield against the uncompromising, black, airless death that surrounded on all sides, gave birth to a strange jurisprudence. In its incipient history the Ring had many of the attributes of a stud farm. The quirks of the legal system from this bygone era were apparent now that the population of the Ring was more than adequate, but by now Terrans had gotten used to their mores, and there was little impetus for change. For example, child support didn't exist on the Ring. Any mother giving birth had three choices regarding her baby. She and the father could register the child as theirs and live happily ever after if both parties so desired. If the father had no interest whatsoever in the baby though and wished to quickly move on to other greener pastures, the State happily acquiesced. The mother could opt to keep the baby herself; if not, the biological resource would be delivered to Child Rearing Services—the biggest governmental agency in existence, anywhere—who were experts in molding unwanted babies into engineers, doctors, scientists, soldiers, craftsmen and anything else required. A sixth of the people living on Terra—around 800 million—began their lives as wards of the State. Terra couldn't do without them.

Contraceptives and abortion both were illegal. The laws against contraception were mostly ignored but the strictures against abortion were vigorously enforced. Maybe the strangest legal quagmire on the Terran Ring related to rape. Granted, one still could find himself in quite a bit of trouble if the woman involved was married, but as far as young, single women were concerned, there was quite a bit of truth in the hundreds of Terran rape jokes that knocked about the Solar System. Terra had thirty-seven degrees of rape—*thirty seven*! It was a lesser offence if the woman had done, or not

34

done, any number of things. The mitigating circumstances were so convoluted and incongruous that even Attila the Hun might have gotten off with but a slap on the wrist. There were fourteen degrees of "enticement" and another twelve of "acquiescence." If the offender was a young, strong, healthy individual who could prove a long line of paternal gifts to the Child Rearing Services, the magistrate would many times make use of a most commonly used catch-all: "unnatural frigidity." The usual penalty was a couple of weeks in mandatory counseling, and these more often than not commonly turned into nothing more than back-slapping sessions. The "thousand before I die" dictum tattooed on Yushenko's and Werth's necks alluded to what Terrans considered the appropriate number of sexual conquests in the contented man's life. All of this made for a rather stunning panorama for a first-time visitor to Terra: millions and millions and millions of women, everywhere, of all ages, and all of them—pregnant. It was actually harder to get used to then the stronger gravity.

Yushenko's chortle was now followed by a slight smirk. The chuckle might have been spontaneous; this monkey-grin was definitely purposeful. It widened the longer Rittener's icy stare was ignored.

"Well, about the gravity," Rittener continued, "I've also wondered if it doesn't also deprive the brain of the necessary blood required to form cogent thoughts?"

Yeshenko's expression changed instantly. He leaned forward, jutting out his square Slavic jaw as if challenging Rittener to swing at this menacing target. He surely wasn't smiling or chuckling now. Whatever he was going to say though was now vetoed by Lieutenant Drake Andrews—Lieutenant, Junior Grade.

"Belay that, Yeshenko." It didn't take a mind-reader to guess that Yeshenko's retort would be better off unsaid. Andrews was always quick with a smile and even after the reprimand managed to purse his thin lips into something that looked like one.

"Captain, I think what is on everyone's mind…" Andrews began.

"I'm not a captain, Lt. Andrews." Rittener cut him off. "In fact, I have no commission whatsoever in the Terran Service."

Andrews was shaking his head. He understood this, of course. "Point well taken. How should we address you?"

Rittener looked again at Yeshenko, and then used his word. "Skipper."

"Skipper it is then." Now Andrew's lips went flat. C-class freighters, smugglers, and pirates had "skippers."

"The point Ensign Gutierrez is making, though, is a valid one. From what I understand, we're not going to be joined by any other force at some point prior to the Asteroid Belt? We're it?"

Rittener's words came out slowly, in a monotone, with as much emotion as someone instructing the mess monitor about the mid-watch meal selections. "There is to be no rendezvous in transit. Our destination is Valerian-3. I just said as much."

Andrews reminded him of his tensor calculus teacher in Shanghai. He was a professor at the Loo Keng-Hua Institute. The European Union picked up quite a hefty stipend to have had such a renowned mathematician tutor the ambassador's son. His teacher had the habit of opening his

36

eyes wide whenever he caught something not quite right in his student's work. "You can't skip steps like that, Clinton," he'd say. "Of course, you have it right, but that is a bad habit. Don't be lazy. Write it out—all of it—step by step. Don't assume I know where you're going. Better that you should be sure yourself then try to impress me with all the math you can do in your head." Ch'in Tsu was dead now, but then so was everyone else Rittener had known on Earth.

Andrews opened his eyes wide like Ch'in Tsu. "So it's just us, then?"

Rittener was tiring of this. He didn't like being cornered into discussing classified orders with a crew member.

"Our actions will be determined by exigencies in the field, Lieutenant. I'm not going to go into anything more specific at this time. I can assure you though that you'll be apprised of everything you need to know, as you need to know it. Until I advise the crew otherwise what I'm now repeating for the third time is that Valerian-3 is our destination, and our mission is to convince that settlement and the rest on the Belt that it's in their interest to abide by the executive order of the Archonate that we're enforcing. You may consider those your orders."

Each man was sizing the other up. Rittener noticed the five stars embroidered above Andrew's name on his tunic— one for each of the five year tours of duty under his belt. Yet there wasn't another single badge or ribbon pinned or sewed anywhere. A fifty-two year old lieutenant—*junior* grade? Could such a thing actually be possible—and if so, were there any others in existence? Rittener's amazement was well-founded; there were only two others in the Service—if the one currently posted to the Virgo Brig awaiting court-martial were counted. Somehow, such a competent imaging specialist such as Andrews had managed a lifetime in the Service and had accrued just a single lousy promotion to show for it.

Andrews was pensively rubbing the crow's feet at the corner of one eye, then moved the index finger to stroke the thin, well-tended mustache. The slight, balding officer had obviously quite a talent for constantly treading water during such a long and undistinguished career. The dogged determination to irritate and alienate anyone who might sign off on the promotions that never came still had not flagged. Andrews pushed on.

"Not to put too fine a point on it then, skipper..." Andrews stopped himself, opened his eyes wide again and asked, "Are we still speaking candidly?"

Rittener nodded affirmatively.

"Well, this ship is hardly anything more than a floating electron laser platform. If we're going into combat, where may I ask, are prisoners going to be held?

Now Yeshenko jumped in with both feet.

"Prisoners?" The laugh that followed was too loud and abrasive to be smoothed over by Lt. Andrews, who just stared at Yeshenko with blank eyes. "Come on, Lieutenant. Even slow-witted, blood-deprived Terrans like us can figure that one out. You know how Earthers fight. Dirt crawlers don't take prisoners."

He turned to Rittener, and in the same tone he used with a drinking buddy called on to settle a boozy debate, invited him to chime in. "You've been in a hundred battles—hell, maybe even a thousand—against dirt crawlers. They ever take one of your guys prisoner?"

Rittener, born and raised on Earth, was himself, of course, a "dirt crawler" too. He had heard the pejorative so many times that its power to sting had long since faded into insignificance. Being labeled one, however, in front of every single crewman on board made it easy for Rittener to choose how he'd couch his next comments.

Rittener withdrew from his waistcoat pocket an impressive-looking document. It was bound in a leather sheathe—*real* leather—and was embossed with the seal of the Terran Archonate, the image inlaid with gold. There were still a few records kept on paper, but it took the crew a moment to recognize what the credentials actually were. Now Rittener was speaking to no one—not Yeshenko nor Andrews nor anyone else really. He was just speaking the words, by law required to be said out loud. He'd planned on making this speech in a perfunctory way, as gentle as possible. He now decided on a different course. He started speaking as he passed the document to Lt. Andrews to verify.

"As per the War Act, section nine, codicil five, and in accordance with the Interplanetary Conventions articles twenty six and twenty seven, I am hereby formally advising all officers and crew of the following. This letter of marque gives absolute and complete authority over the ship *Peerless* to the holder of this marque. Any and all orders given by the holder of this letter shall be lawfully and strictly obeyed by any and all Terran crew and/or passengers aboard the *Peerless*."

He paused. "You'll sign that please, Mr. Andrews, and then pass it to Ensign Gutierrez." Noticing that the lieutenant was at sea regarding how this old-fashioned paper and pen stuff went, he slid a handsome stylograph which even worked in zero gravity across the desk to him. "Your signature, at the bottom, by your name." He then went on.

"The holder of this marque is granted the authority to pursue the legitimate interests of the Terran Archonate in dealings with its enemies in whatever manner the holder deems necessary, prudent and efficient, subject to the above mentioned interplanetary conventions."

While Ensign Gutierrez was reading and signing the letter, Seaman Werth came to an overjoyed epiphany.

"Gott im himmel! I'm on a pirate ship!" He slapped his friend's muscled back. "We're damned pirates now, Yushenko—and with double pay and a promotion waiting for us when we get back to the Ring! Ah...and I was the German donkey too stupid to know that no one with a whit of sense volunteered for anything, no? What do you say now?"

Rittener gave him a real smile, showing a perfect set of teeth. Of course no teeth could be *that* perfect, but nineteen of them were actually real; the rest were lost in countless battles. His eyes lit up listening to Werth's blunt translation of the letter of marque. Well, the green one lit up anyway, not the blue one. There were so many parts of Rittener's body that were biosynthetic that he himself had long forgotten what it felt like to have been at one time in one single piece. The biosynthetic eye had over the years changed from the original green to aqua blue. This was not unusual and there were remedies for it. Rittener just opted to leave it as it was.

Gutierrez made to hand the document back to Rittener, but he waved her off. "Seaman Werth, you're absolutely correct. This isn't a Terran ship; this is my ship." And with that he dropped the other shoe. "Ensign Gutierrez, please count the number of 'up to and including the penalty of death' admonitions in that document. The number escapes me now."

Rittener wasn't smiling now. He looked like a Celtic warrior—after a long, hard, lost battle. Or perhaps a closer approximation, especially with the long, swooping, ochre mustache, would be a tough trooper of the 7th Cavalry. His blonde hair was parted in the middle and fell to his collar. It was straight and very fine and hadn't receded in the least. That feature was boyish still, unlike very much else about him. Having called various purgatories his home since his youth, and surrounded by the denizens of these cruel precincts, he had allowed himself to be influenced by them. His face was long, narrowing to a blunt jaw and accentuated with a meandering, deep scar that ran from his left cheek bone to the cleft in his chin. In Rittener's profession, as with 19th Century students in duel-crazed Prussia, scars were almost prized and it was far from rare to forego having them cosmetically erased. The eyes though, in Rittener's case, were almost hypnotic. The green one, the real one, still reflected a virtuous humanity, an eye that seemed to want to shed tears for what it had seen. The blue one warned of another side, a dead side, one that had seen very little other than ruin and destruction.

The only sound in the room was that of Gutierrez nervously flipping through the paperwork, her agitated hands rustling the document. After what seemed an interminable duration, she answered bluntly. "Six, Sir."

Rittener moved his eyes slowly from crewman to crewman as he spoke. His reputation had preceded him, as he well knew, and he now brought that weapon to bear. "This isn't a Terran ship; this is *my* ship. I will personally execute every single crewman, if I have to, and send the

Peerless spiraling into the Sun before I'll see a single one of my orders disobeyed." It wasn't anxiety or fear or outrage or any other emotion he saw reflected back in their eyes; it was utter shock.   As if what he'd just said to the crew was nothing out of the ordinary, as if he'd made a bland comment about the weather or some other mundane topic, he simply moved on to close the meeting. "I'll summon each of you individually to discuss the particulars of your specialties and how I want things run in short order. Unless there are any other questions, you are all dismissed."

The whole crew sat frozen, no one knowing just exactly what to make of what had just happened. Rittener seemed slightly irritated with their discomfiture and broke the spell by waving his hand and repeating "dismissed." As the crew silently started to respond he over-ruled himself, as if suddenly remembering an afterthought.

"Oh, one more thing. Mr. Findlay, place Seaman 2nd class Yeshenko under arrest and escort him to the brig."

With that one off-handed remark Rittener turned his entire crew to stone just as surely and quickly as if he'd shown them all the head of Medusa. Now a *truly* interminable and deathly silence descended. Rittener was looking down at his letter of marque, checking to see that all was in order, so he wasn't taking in the looks of astonishment on the faces of his flabbergasted crew. Findlay, though, reacted automatically. He pulled himself up, put his meat hook hands on his hips, and gave Yeshenko a gruff order.

"On your feet, Seaman."

The tartar Yeshenko slowly obeyed but while fixing Rittener with a deadly stare and slowly nodding his head as if affirming a stream of unspoken yet toxic thoughts within.

42

Chief Warrant Officer Findlay was the security officer—a barrel-chested sailor who resembled a bear as much as a man. An impossibly thick and grizzled, dark brown beard exploded in every direction from his massive face. Two deep furrows ran on either side of his substantial, alcohol-ravaged snout of a nose, disappearing into the wiry tangle below. The Welshman had been a boxer in a past life; when he told people to get on their feet, the sane ones always complied. Yeshenko was sane enough to obey but was tarrying, still playing at sending visual daggers in Rittener's direction.

"Let's go, Yeshenko. You heard the skipper." He motioned to the hatch with one of his bear claws.

As they were exiting Rittener gave a final order. "He's to be held 'hard,' Chief. Seventy-two hours. The charge is 'overt contempt.' Log it."

Held 'hard' was simplicity itself. The offender was just stuffed into a stainless steel compartment the size of a closet and forgotten for a while. The only amenities were a miniature commode and a quarter inch tube that gave out a weak stream of drinking water when pressure was applied. That was it though. No food, feeble light, not a sound worth listening to, no nothing; it was meant to be three days of hell.

All in all, Rittener thought to himself as the crew exited in silence, the voyage could have gotten off to a better start. But, then again, he reminded himself, it could have been worse.

Chapter Three

The Fair Sport

"What *are* you playing at?" Nerissa had rudely asked him just before the match began.

It was an old habit of his, good or bad isn't to say, just like the scholars and wits of the Old Modern seem to have done, of giving out with Latin truisms and sayings. A few of them, people thought, were going to go down in history. Pan-Turkic insurgents, for example, once had him surrounded in the Fergana Valley near Samarkand. Their pitiless warlord, Tevfik Bey, called a cease-fire for a last minute parley. He shared some disheartening information with Rittener, namely that his forces had commandeered a Fung Shang military class satellite which he now threatened to turn loose on Rittener's positions in the valley below. He advised surrender in blunt terms. "You haven't any way out," the warlord told him.

"Aut viam inveniam aut faciam," Rittener had replied. Rittener waited just the right amount of time. "That's Caesar or Hannibal, it could be either. It means 'I'll find a way, or else make one.'"

He knew most people didn't like being schooled this way. He intended that effect though more often than not. She was no Tevfik Bey, but Rittener thought she deserved a shot across her bow too.

"Verba competitorem verum non volant, facta sua manent," he told her. Rittener waited just the right amount of time. "That's Horace or Virgil, I'm not sure which. It means 'A master gamesman's words don't fly, but rather his deeds remain.' Good flying, Nerissa."

Even she had to appreciate the quick cleverness of the double entendre. "Good flying" was the standard polite salute to fellow pilots prior to a match. It actually shut her right up; Latin did that much of the time.

Now just moments before the contest would start, Rittener set to preparing himself. He took an extended series of long, deep, rhythmic breaths, filling his lungs with the cast off oxygen from both the tailings of crushed and vaporized lunar regolith and the exhalations of the millions of plants and trees in the Garden. It definitely didn't taste like air on Earth. But it was thick—dense enough to fly in, especially in one sixth gravity. He tried not to concentrate on anything but his breathing and stretching right now, but the panorama before him made that impossible. If a view of the Terran Ring was the iconic image of humanity, Borealis from the top of the Epsilon Ring presented a good case for a very close second.

The topography of the Traskett Crater resembled an Assyrian shield—flat, round, and with a long, thick spike protruding from the center. It's strategic position so close to the lunar North Pole made for the most efficient and secure ingress and egress, and kept it *just* out of clear sight of the Sun, or Terra. The fields around Borealis had been suffused with the richest deposits of helium-3 on the Moon, or anywhere else. Billions of tons of the purest ice—pristine, untouched, lying frozen at the bottom of craters which hadn't seen the Sun since the Solar System was young—was at hand nearby. With all this, it was foreordained that a great city should rise here.

The "Core" was the hollowed out "spike" on the shield. It was the Old City, the original habitation from Settlement Times—a rock-hewn labyrinth now used for other purposes and stocked with food, oxygen, fuel and every other vital necessity. It was enough to last Borealis, well, no one knew how long, save the Council itself. In the worst of circumstances, should Borealis' dome be ruptured, the city could certainly hold out long enough to affect repairs. That had never happened but people naturally never seemed to tire talking about what would happen if it did.

Around the Core, ring by ring, level by level, Borealis rose from the ground, wrapped around the exterior of the jutting protuberance in the lunar crust. It spiraled up twenty-seven levels. Each of these was named but the city's five Districts were designated by the places where the Core tapered dramatically—Alpha to Epsilon. Borealis, therefore, looked quite a bit like ancient illustrations of the Tower of Babel, only this one was as real as the geysers of Enceladus orbiting around Saturn. Awash in what had been a virtual sea of helium-3, Borealis was rich too—rich beyond description. The wealthiest on Borealis, people were at first surprised to learn, were members of the Artists' Guild. A certified master could command a wage from Borealis' glitterati that even Croesus himself might have had trouble paying. Borelians were so rich though that there wasn't much else on which to spend their credits. Even after the mind-boggling flood of imports from all over the Solar

System were paid for, the surplus wealth had no place else to go. The State started it all—decorating all the public buildings, every square foot of them, with stunning bas-reliefs carved into the exterior facades. Private citizens were quickly infected and now it was the rare domicile that wasn't faced with the most breath-taking murals. The most affluent residents fashioned theirs in pure gold, silver or copper. The motifs were scenes from every terrestrial mythology, watershed events in history, reproductions of the marvels of the Solar System—and anything else one could imagine, or *couldn't* imagine. The Titan Consortium, to give just one example, had opted for a work depicting the Rings of Saturn. To represent the detritus swirling around that gas giant, tens of thousands of diamonds, rubies and sapphires had been inlaid in a monolithic slab of pure black titanium. There were many others equally as awe-inspiring: Phidippides running to Athens after Marathon, Columbus landing in the Americas, Adam and Eve in the Garden of Eden. Each domicile fit cheek to jowl with the next, creating a series of spectacularly decorated toruses built into the Core, stacked one atop another, all the way up to Epsilon.

It was next to impossible to visit Borealis for simple pleasure. Tourism had long since been out of the question. If the floodgates were opened a stampede of billions would ensue, trampling to dust this jewel of humanity by virtue of the weight alone. There was plenty of everything on Borealis, but for a quarter million, not one hundred billion. To receive official permission from Customs for transit wasn't just rare, it was the surest proof that one was indeed among the few of the most powerful and important persons alive. The best-selling "Declined"—beamed everywhere and setting sales records year after year—catalogued the jaw-dropping list of people to whom the Borelians had flatly said "no." In perusing the list of princes, gold-medalists, politicians and magnates who'd been turned down, the reader was constrained to ask himself what chance *he* had. And the answer was simple: none. Such hopeless folly even entered the lexicon. Teachers from Earth to the Outer scolded their daydreaming students not by asking them if they were on "Cloud Nine," but now more often if they were "strolling on Borealis."

A noteworthy footnote to the tortuous process of acquiring a valid Borelian visa was that after all the documentation required, after an itinerary submitted accurate to the minute, when it *was* approved it always stipulated a transit time thirty-six hours in advance of the duration requested. Such a generous but seemingly incongruous boon made sense though. It would have been inhuman to allow anyone on Borealis without giving them time to take the city in with their own eyes. Borelians had no trouble spotting the few august visitors in their midst, and not just from the fact that the average human was much shorter and very much thicker. The residents took some pleasure in watching chubby, stunned Terrans and Earthers stumbling through their streets on feet unaccustomed to the light gravity, open-mouthed and yet dumb-struck. If one stripped the frieze from Trajan's Column and wrapped it in precious metals and jewelry around a five layer wedding cake, and were it then made large enough to accommodate two hundred thousand, this would be Borealis. No better prelude could be imagined before an important conference with adversaries and competitors than simply by giving the visiting diplomats and businessmen some free time to take in the sights of the city.

"So, how do you find Borealis?" The Council never opened their discussions any other way, knowing of course that their visitors would be quite speechless to answer.

This was just the treasure they squandered on the aesthetics of the city though. Borealis' true wealth and power was the result of almost two centuries of sheer determination that had transformed the Lunar North Pole into the single most important power source fueling the entire Solar System. And all that lie outside the Dome.

Borealis knew nothing but spring days. It was ironic that there existed no night in the place that put the goddess of the Moon and the night on their seals. Thousands of stupendous mirrors ringed the Traskett Crater, beaming sunlight to the floor below. The mirrors' degree of curvature, placement and height had been carefully calculated to both catch the maximum sunlight throughout the year and refract the concentrated rays into widened and weakened beams that bathed beneficent light over great swaths on the crater floor. It was well-named: the Goldilocks Array. It should naturally be a couple hundred degrees below zero on the Traskett floor, and it *was* a couple hundred degrees above zero Fahrenheit over the lip of the crater in the direct sunlight. Inside the Dome though, thanks to Goldilocks, everything was "just right." Not all the mirrors could be used all the time owing to Luna's dance with her celestial partners, Sun and Earth. But with gradual and automated re-focusing, thanks to the Moon's polar phenomenon of constant sunlight at least at some nearby horizon, there was never-ending dayglow in abundance. If "night-hungry" Borelians complained of it from time to time, the plants never did.

Old jokes about Borelian cuisine—built on a "truism" of long by-gone days—a lot of time fell flat. "I don't get it," many would say after some head-scratching. Some old-timer would have to explain.

"I've tasted 'goop'—the real stuff. Honestly," many an aged mossback would attest.

Some wag would almost certainly cast doubt on that. "And wasn't it your great, great, great, grandfather that was shot at by Pancho Villa? Or was it by Ganymedean pirates out around the moons of Jupiter?" Long-toothed veterans who still possessed their wits knew such avowals could easily attract mockery and were prepared for it.

Whether true or false, everyone though loved a good goop story, everyone wanted to know what it tasted like. The effective story-teller was the one who could enliven the tale with appropriate faces; they named it "goop" for a reason.

In Settlement Times anything that could be chewed and swallowed was eaten, that part is true. With goop though chewing wasn't required. It came in a wide variety of cheerful colors, each indicating from which family of plants the mush had been concocted. There's no supposing that one couldn't get used to it because Borelians had indeed eaten it for many, many years. Believe it or not, some Borelians ate it still, on occasion, just for the novelty, it was assumed. But there were some that sincerely professed that they enjoyed it.

The canard that the first pioneers existed on it though is a great fiction. In truth, goop was little more than a footnote in Borelian history as even in the first years terrestrial crops were grown using pathetic forerunners of Goldilocks. No one ate heartily in those first primitive days but neither did they dine on goop exclusively either. Yet even the Old City museum was happy to play along. The restaurant there served thirty-three varieties. Goop wasn't born of necessity, but rather of other purely human attributes: boredom, curiosity, and the need for diversion. Would it be possible, settlers had asked themselves, to produce "indigenous" lunar food, comestibles that could be grown nowhere else but on the Moon? Botanists, gardeners, cooks and hobbyists in the Old City were determined to find out. They rigged hermetically sealed planters with the genetically-engineered offspring of quite bizarre hybrids—utilizing the gene pool of the most resilient plants. After fits and starts and trials and errors, the hardiest of these plant monsters were placed in the blistering sunlight, shielded to a degree by well-designed solar panels that at least blocked most of the ultraviolet and some of the rest of the scorching rays. Clever water-fed heat exchangers bled off some of the intense temperatures, but these mutants nonetheless had to survive in environments that reached 170° F. Each hobbyist had his own highly-guarded secrets to protect—the just perfect percentage of carbon dioxide in the ambience being the most hotly debated. The mature plants were ingeniously processed with synthetic emulsifiers and taste additives, and boiled into a bland paste that was extruded and served. It was eaten hot, cold, frozen, fried—even broiled in the Sun—but try as one might, it always tasted like, well, what it was: goop.

Goldilocks was built to heat and light Borealis, yes, but that was always just a side benefit. It's *raison d'etre* was to convert the regolith out from the Dome to a boundary near the periphery of the crater walls into a lush cornucopia. A good portion of the Traskett crater's outer margins though were of no use. To go past the Shadow Line was the same as to go over the lip into the direct sun; it was certain death if unprotected. From the circumference of the Shadow Line then to the periphery of the Dome a roughly circular, transparent dextrite lid was erected, suspended on steel struts. This let the ceaseless and tempered reflected sunlight through, kept out the vacuum of space, and held in the carbon dioxide rich micro-atmosphere. Fruits, vegetables, grains, herbs, spices and other flora of every conceivable type thrived below in a fantastic version of the Late Carboniferous period of Old Earth, the carbon dioxide levels only restrained by what the bees could tolerate. The bounty this green carpet gave forth was more than sufficient for Borealis, along with blessing the city with tons of clean oxygen and soaking up the exhaled breaths of thousands to convert to sugars. Borelian cuisine was actually then quite delicious and particularly healthy. The "Garden" not only made the jokes much harder to tell, it was also exemplary of yet another wedge driven between the peoples of the Inner. The culture of death was on Earth and Terra, not here in peaceful, vivacious Borealis. No animal had ever been butchered legally since Settlement Times and they meant to keep it that way. It was a tangible and sanguine proof that they—and not the other cultures of the Inner—that they were the enlightened entities into which humanity had been meant to evolve.

Beyond the Garden lay the rest of the Moon—the "Field." It was the piston at the center of the engine that was Borealis. The tracts adjacent to the Traskett crater had been exploited from the very first stage of primitive human colonization, pushing out prodigious quantities of helium-3. Nothing goes on forever though, and it was no secret that these fields, along with others even further out from Borealis, had long since approached the end of their productive life. Earth and Terra were much more anxious about this than the Borelians themselves who mined and exported it. There were other fields to be tapped, they'd answer calmly. Granted, the best potential sites were the equatorial fields some 1,500 miles away. Undaunted by the distance, Borealis was making preparations to plant her flag and her robotic regolith skimmers into this virgin territory and stubbornly maintained that the current pinch in supply need not precipitate a crisis in the future, as long as the correct steps were taken now. Terra and Earth were just as convinced that the opposite were true and that the helium-3 shortfall was more than just the current state of affairs, that it was the opening chapter of an endemic problem that everyone in the Solar System had been dreading, and from which too many eyes had looked away for too long. Borealis was trying to open these new fields as quickly as possible but there were plenty of interests who determined that this pace wasn't good enough.

The politics of helium-3 was the great question of the day. Prospectors, miners and speculators called it "atomic gold"—AG for short. It pushed to the fore many nagging questions that all parties in the Inner had procrastinated in answering, assuming that things would take care of themselves. They hadn't, of course. And now there were a number of grey areas that were threatening to turn blood red. Who *did* own the Moon, anyway? Certainly, no one refused to recognize Borealis' sovereignty and control of areas she already developed and mined. But where was it written that she owned the *whole* Moon? She had soaked up incalculable wealth from all quadrants of the Solar System for centuries, but must such greed and self-interest extend forever into eternity?

Earth and Terra both considered the Field "terra incognita" and saw no reason why their considerable muscle shouldn't be brought to bear to increase the supply of helium-3. Having her customers help themselves to Luna's helium-3 on their own was an idea that held few Borelian adherents. Dante Michelson, the fire-breathing Chief Archon of Terra was well-known to the Borelians, thanks to his prior office as Terra's ambassador to the city. Michelson was a hard-liner and had his reasons for the extreme opinions. Like most "ambassadors" he had been first and foremost a spy, and through his network of contacts was in a position to see and hear things like few others. In short, he believed the Borelians were lying—plain and simple. He thought they'd been lying for years. Even though Borealis hadn't advertised the equatorial fields as a bonanza, he suspected that their potential yield had been purposefully exaggerated and that the speedy timetable which would infuse the market with additional supplies was hardly more than fantasy. Finally, he knew what this all meant, thinking four or five steps ahead as he always had. It was ironic that it was his signature on the accord that put the hard questions off a few more years. The Field was legally neither Borealis' nor was it terra incognita, which would have left it open to anyone. By interplanetary law it currently lurked in the limbo of "disputed territory." But he'd signed that as the ambassador of a previous regime. He was no ambassador now. As Chief Archon of the Terran Ring he was the most powerful man in the Solar System, and in his mind it *was* terra incognita.

The helium-3 was running out. That was the plain fact. For many in the know both in the Inner and the Outer it was an obvious reality that wasn't up for debate. The only question was if this new energy crisis would spawn horrific wars like the last one. The four Petroleum Wars of the Old Modern made the World Wars of the 20th Century seem like polite skirmishes. Would history repeat itself? The pragmatists on Terra and Earth thought so. The laws of supply and demand were as impossible to disobey as Newton's Laws of Motion. Where helium-3 was concerned the demand was increasing relentlessly and as for the supply, well, as with petroleum, it had long since ceased being created.

Helium-3 had been delivered to the Moon via the solar wind, blasted into the airless, defenseless lunar surface amid an angry stream of alpha particles hurled at the Moon over four billion years. Earth's magnetic shield prevented this gift of the Sun from being deposited on the home planet and it couldn't be obtained anywhere else. Yes, for the benefit of sticklers, there might be stores on Neptune and Uranus, but so what? No one considered the kind of Herculean efforts that would be required to get at *that* supply, especially when the Moon was such a close and relatively friendly and benign place. It was mined so simply and easily too on the Moon: it was just scooped up by robotic regolith skimmers. The top few inches of the lunar surface was scraped up, vaporized by solar collectors, and the liberated gas obtained. Exporting it to Terra and Earth was even easier. Canisters of pressurized helium-3 were loaded like ammunition in the breeches of Materials Export Cannons with 800 yard long barrels. These "pea shooters" couldn't have been erected on Earth, and along with the Goldilocks Array, would have collapsed under their own colossal weight. But as Borelians reminded everyone, "Nothing is impossible on the Moon." These behemoths fired projectiles at escape velocity—only around a kilometer per second on Luna—fast enough to overcome the Moon's gentle gravity and non-existent air drag, and sent the cargo on to Earth orbit for eager customers. Fusion reactors, by the thousands, powered mankind's universe and helium-3 was the fuel that fed those reactors. No more simple equation existed.

Elementary physics said that the Moon's equator should be loaded with helium-3; more complicated physics gave some answers as to why it wasn't. Sunlight striking the lunar equator was ferocious and packed with helium-3 ions stripped of electrons. If mother lodes of the stuff should be found around the Lunar North Pole where the light struck so much more obliquely, the common wisdom was that there should be astounding quantities yet to be mined in the equatorial regions. Sadly, that was not the case. There was a controversy raging about why that was.

Opinions were changing about the relative weakness and duration of the Moon's ancient magnetic field. There were many respected scholars who had very plausible evidence that it had been a real force in the ancient past—deflecting the solar wind and depriving Luna's equator and temperate zones of helium-3 while at the same time funneling the concentrated stream straight to the place where great quantities had already been found—the Lunar North Pole. Further, it was seen now that the alpha particles weren't just deposited on the Moon like rain falling on the surface of Earth's continental prairies to be soaked up by the sod. The mineral composition of each site played a very significant role in the calculus of absorption and retention. Depending on the chemistry and geology involved the precious motes could penetrate too deeply, too erratically, fail to be captured, or even if suffused originally might not be held for billions of years awaiting the robotic scoops of human mining operations. What those mineral and geologic hallmarks were was the most highly-guarded secret of the Council. There *were* fields yet to be mined, but they were scattered all over Luna. And even though Borealis wasn't speaking plainly about it anymore, from the reserved communiqués issued about the matter from time to time it was fairly obvious that the good old days of AG flowing in abundance from the Moon were quickly coming to an end.

But what about the Lunar *South* Pole? It hadn't been touched. Granted, without a single crystal of ice to be found in the whole expanse it would be hard sledding to get a real operation up and running there. Surely though, with the price of AG what it was, it would make sense any way one looked at it. The Borelians *had* looked at it—long, long ago—and had come away shaking their heads.

A great scientific dispute raged about the Lunar South Pole. For the Borelians there was no mystery about it. If conspiracy theorists wished to peddle their rumors about vast stores, secret mining ventures and all the rest, the Borelians couldn't be bothered with it. Their prospectors had surveyed the area meticulously. There wasn't any AG there.

The Aitken Basin straddles the Lunar South Pole. It's one of the largest craters in the entire Solar System—2,500 kilometers across. The Leibnitz Mountains ring the crater, named for the co-discoverer of calculus, Isaac Newton's great rival. Much of what was thought to be known about the Aitken Basin changed after the Borelian survey was released. The ripples caused by the bombshells within the survey reports crashed against a watershed in Borelian history; they censor now even non-strategic discoveries. Prior astrophysical assumptions about the Aitken Basin were just simply in error, the reports made clear. Scientists had always guessed at the age of around 3.8 billion years for the crater. Borealis now had proof that the guess had been off—way off. Radiometric age-dating techniques were a sure way to tell the last time the surface of the basin had been molten. The surveyors had no doubt after checking when those geologic clocks within the lunar regolith had been melted and reset. The Aitken Crater wasn't age-old, it was actually quite young. They determined that the object that struck came in at a low angle—around 30 degrees—striking a glancing blow that didn't dig in so much as scrape away. This object still packed quite a punch—blasting into space the top layer of the Lunar South Pole to a depth of 13 kilometers. The event occurred not 3.8 billion years ago but rather at some time within the last half billion years. This accounted for the dearth of helium-3. Whatever had walloped the Moon had hit it in the chin hard enough to knock its beard off. If the Lunar South Pole had been soaking up helium-3 since the dawn of the Solar System that treasure was lost forever, having been jettisoned into space along with everything else within the erstwhile surface of the Lunar South Pole.

"We're looking at the scene of the greatest theft in the history of mankind," the party chief of the survey crew told the news services. "There's no broken glass or splintered door, but the AG is missing and the only thing left is this enormous hole." His assistant was more philosophical. "One asteroid snuffs out the dinosaurs and opens the door for our existence, another robs us of what possibly could have been half of our helium-3 supply." She shrugged her shoulders over the "spilled milk" that she called it. "I'd say our batting average isn't that bad."

"Spilled milk" might have been the wrong analogy though. One distinguished economist who certainly was crying over it estimated that if the reserves lost were anything like those of the Lunar North Pole, it represented an amount of credits sufficient to buy quite a sizeable homestead: North America.

Whether or not the economist had his astronomical figures correct, the ridiculous price of helium-3 had risen to undreamed of prices and as such was the standard complaint of everyone, from barbers on Terra to chicken farmers on Earth. It was playing havoc with the economy of the entire Solar System. The party line on Borealis was that there was no need to panic and that steps were underway to put everything right. Dante Michelson on Terra knew otherwise and so did Clinton Rittener. As one of the most famed *condottieri* of Earth, he was several steps up from just an average mercenary. He had a few contacts of his own.

Rittener had the corner of his eye on his Terran rival two pads to his left. Demetrius Sehene was stretching and breathing too. But he wasn't directing a single furtive glance at the competition. He was the odds on favorite to win the match and one look at him told why. His Bulgarian father was the gold-medalist champion wrestler of the Inner Games XXXII. The seed hadn't fallen far. He was tall, superbly built, and as solid as spent uranium. This formidable clay was molded by the features he inherited from his Tutsi mother, along with also taking her family's name. Long-tendoned, quick-firing musculature so prevalent among that tribe had been fine tuned and tempered by intense training. His tawny skin and Abyssinian nose caused people to remark that he looked like the old Ethiopian emperor, Haile Selassie. Demetrius liked that and played it up. His fans referred to him just as "The Emperor"; the moniker fit perfectly.

World-class piloting required a body like Demitrius'. Every amateur who visited Borealis tried doing it though and anyone in decent health and shape could keep it up for a while. The beginners' platforms were fairly safe, although if one were clumsy enough to make a determined attempt it was possible to break one's neck even at these tame heights. Piloting was basically a struggle against one's own body, a marathon work-out session that pushed the flyer to the point where the arms told the brain that nothing more could be endured. While that point came at a different place for every pilot, the math however was the same for all. To effect flight on the Moon one had to continuously flap long, broad wings with the force equal to one tenth body weight as measured on Earth. A two-hundred pound man, for example, doing "flys" in a gymnasium on Earth with 20 pound dumbbells could fly on the Moon. All he need do is put down the weights and strap on the wings.

Piloting was considered the "fair sport" because anyone could do it—children, women, men. The competition was fair because the bigger you were the harder you had to push to keep your weight aloft. Accomplished fliers though were easily recognized by the hallmark shared by all: admirably developed, V-shaped torsos topped by massive shoulders and arms. It was inevitable that Terrans should come to overthrow the Borelians as the dominant force in the sport.

They were stronger—how else to put it? The first match lost to them came as a shock to Borealis nonetheless. When it started to happen regularly the shock turned to dismay. Piloting was as Borelian as goop, and here the Terrans had commandeered yet another piece of their culture. The Borelians were no push-overs, though. Watching a trained Borelian pilot was wondrous indeed. Their tall, lithe, lean form was made for the sport. What the light gravity took from their strength it reimbursed by permitting longer limbs that changed the calculus of leverage in their favor. Their other advantage was disputed by the Terrans. It was a fact though. Borelians were better pilots. They grew up flying and were such agile, daring, practiced pilots that they gave Terra's best a hotly-contested run for their money every time they met.

A colossal holographic torus switched on. It fit snugly into the upper reaches of the Dome, a concentric virtual racetrack, its imaginary center the spire atop the Epsilon Observation Deck. Each pilot wore ankle bands that must remain within the volume of the virtual doughnut and a collar that likewise would immediately disqualify the wearer should he fly too high or too low. The wings were tipped with similar sensors—wings, one might point out, of the lightest material ever constructed. Most were fashioned with arcane genres of carbon fibers, but there were many trade secrets connected to the manufacture of the best wings.

The torus turned yellow; the pilots took their marks. Every voice in Borealis was shouting encouragement to the tense pilots. Rittener could hear a good number of brave voices screaming, "Good flying, Clinton!" Rittener always professed that he flew for himself alone, that he represented no one but himself. But his skin-tight, blue and red piloting leotard, the colors of the European Union, said otherwise. The old planet below might be in shambles but here was one son of Earth at least not quite ready to say die. The cheers made him glad that he'd decided to sport these colors; that was his last thought before the torus turned light-green.

The pilots leaped into the air en masse and flew at top speed toward the torus. There was little room for maneuver at this point of the race; most pilots just clenched their teeth and literally beat their way through with their wings. There *were* some vague rules in piloting, but not at the start, not really. During the "scrum" no judge ever threw a flag. It was pure aerial combat and almost anything went. Some beat their way through to the goal of the torus, others spiraled out either injured or with damaged wings, still others didn't make it within the confines of the holographic racetrack in time. Rittener didn't try anything tricky and flew straight at the closest sector of the torus. So did many other pilots. Converging vectors resulted in a number of "tangles" settled in the air as birds of prey would resolve them, with kicks and buffeting wings.

Nerissa wasn't among them. She opted for a daring stratagem, flying at a recklessly wide angle, trying to intersect the torus far down the course. While her competitors were making a straight bee-line for the track, Nerissa would have to traverse the much longer hypotenuse she'd chosen for her bearing—but in the same time. Demetrius had taken an angle too but nothing so audacious as Nerissa's. Already the torus was blinking on and off at an alarming rate. By the time Nerissa's wing tips passed the virtual boundary it was flashing like a strobe light. Then it switched suddenly to a dark green. Any pilots' sensors outside the safe boundary instantly lit up red. They were out. Nerissa had made it with but a second or two to spare and her gambling short cut put her far ahead of the pack. Fearless confidence in her amazing speed was matched by graceful agility which had her hugging the extreme inside of the ethereal race course—"in the groove." But Demetrius was hard on her heels, coming up fast at a gentle angle of intersection, beating the air like a winged demon fleeing Hell. Just before the two vectors crossed Nerissa banked out of the groove and heeled into Demetrius' path. It was a first-class impact. Surprised cries rippled through the crowd looking up breathlessly. Now a real "tangle" ensued, with each pilot trying to maintain speed while blocking the other, and desperately attempting to force the other to dip wings outside of the safe boundary. This was nasty flying, indeed.

Three circuits around the track were required before a pilot made his headlong "dive" to the finish line, a checkered holographic tape floating above Kepler's Arch. Nerissa and Demetrius confronted each other again and again over the three laps, frittering away both speed and distance in the lead in an astounding number of tangles, only diverting attention on each other when the pack caught up with them. The two best pilots in existence then broke away, gained a comfortable margin, and resumed another series of feints, blocks, pushes and crashes. This was nasty flying, indeed.

Rittener was out of the race. Oh, he'd made it out of the scrum in time and was still alive, technically. But he was flying way out of his league. He had never really had a chance and was pleased that he'd been able to maintain a decent position in the middle of the pack that chased after the front runners. The spectacle Nerissa and Demetrius were putting on helped him in a way. Their aerial dogfights were enough to take Rittener's focus off the burning lactic acid that was building up in his arms and shoulders.

The two combatants reached the terminus of the third lap a fraction of a second apart. This was bad news for Demetrius; no pilot dived like Nerissa. As a matter of fact, not even Nerissa was supposed to be able to fly like Nerissa. Physicists had made detailed studies—plugging in her height and weight, the counteracting forces of lift, gravity, torque and everything else—and the conclusion was that her airborne exploits were just simply…impossible. Her hallmark dives though were nothing less than superhuman. Both pilots skimmed the absolute virtual inside boundary of the race course at the third lap post. Both wheeled to dive and tangled wickedly, like two raptors locking talons in mid-air, whirling and falling. Demetrius broke away and effected a near-vertical swoop for the finish line. For Nerissa's fans, banking on her patented sprint, disaster struck. She wasn't sprinting, she wasn't diving, she wasn't even flying. She was gliding down in a gentle, defeated spiral, barely pumping her wings. She was quite obviously injured.

Demetrius Sehene flew through the finish line like a peregrine falcon, to the accompaniment of a furious cascade of booing that rose up from the city and reverberated off the Dome. A throng of Borelians crowded around the panel of judges, crying foul and gesticulating angrily. The judges were making a good show of ignoring them, leaning together in for what all the world looked like an unbiased consultation. They decided quickly. The holographic torus turned red again indicating that the race was over. There is no "second place" in piloting, or any other place, only winning. "Demetrius Sehene: WINNER!" was flashed across the race course now emptying of dozens of also-rans, in letters as high as terrestrial skyscrapers.

Rittener glided to solid ground at Alpha so spent he could barely summon the energy to shake out the pools of sweat that flooded his eyes, blurring his vision. Giant, lethargic drops of perspiration—bloated by the lunar gravity and falling in slow motion—came flying off him in every direction as he shook out his sweat-soaked hair. When he could finally focus he saw the scene before him was almost pandemonium. Borelians, always reserved, once pushed to their limits *could* react very emotionally. The makings of a riot were all around him. Even the attendants were ranting and raving, oblivious to the fact that *someone* ought to have helped unbuckle Rittener's wings. He didn't really care that much though and just stood where he landed, panting, his arms quivering. Security officers were roughly pushing and threatening a path through the mob, half-dragging a stunned Demetrius Sehene through the opening they created. Nerissa was herself surrounded by a cordon of security and medical staff. She was rubbing her left shoulder with one hand, but used the other to wave off the solicitous physicians who seemed determined to attend to her.

Suddenly they made eye-contact, he ignored, his wings dragging on the ground; she, surrounded like a queen-bee, quite sated but yet being offered royal jelly by courtiers who were hard-wired to think of nothing else. Their eyes locked for quite some time, long enough for Rittener to read her expression doubtlessly. It wasn't the face of dejection or defeat, nor did it radiate pain or anger. Clinton Rittener had saved millions of lives and had sent millions of others to their deaths by reading faces.

He was an expert at it—if anyone was.

Chapter Four

The Bacalar Device

Sadhana Ramanujan wasn't exactly *persona non grata* with the Terran Archonate but neither was she invited to many of their holiday celebrations. Her views were too liberal and her mouth a little too open. But she was a descendant of *that* Ramanujan, which her father had never let her forget. And she *had* lived up to her illustrious Indian ancestor—Swrinivasa Ramanujan, one of the great mathematical savants of the 20th Century. Her ancestor was a genius who not only mastered higher mathematics as a child, but who was discovering new trigonometric theorems—by the age of twelve! Sadhana means "long practiced." With her father pushing relentlessly from a young age and the string of important postulates she'd discovered herself, she couldn't have been more aptly named. Her breakthrough innovation of increasing the nanoscale cooling effect in graphene chips (only one atom thick!) catapulted nanocomputing into the next level and beyond. Heat had been the biggest obstacle in performance, a barrier which she hurdled in front of the astounded and grateful hundreds of billions from Earth to Titan. Sadhana Ramanujan had doubled the speed of the System at a stroke, changing history. It would be difficult to say then whether the Terran Archonate or Sadhana Ramanujan were honored more by the request the Archonate sent her, or by Ramanujan's decision to drop everything and comply.

She'd been here before, of course. Standing in the foyer in front of the Archonate's massive portal the same feeling as before came over her. It was meant to impress anyone with a pair of eyes and it rarely disappointed. Sadhana saw something else though in the outlandishly oversize set of solid steel doors. They reminded her of the images of the Second World War she'd seen, of the massive 20 foot high mahogany and marble doors to the Fuhrer's private office. There was little subtlety in Terran architecture. Beyond this threshold lay the greatest single power in the known Universe. That's what the intimidating style and design said and that was thought to be enough.

She was met by a very high-ranking staffer of the Archonate and two security officers, all smiling and exchanging greetings, while forming a protective cocoon around her and whisking her through a beehive of activity. The Archonate was cavernous—the biggest single office space on the Ring. It went from Ground all the way up to the Exterior Decks, occupying an arc that stretched for miles. Her party commandeered an entire shuttle and was gently whisked toward the epicenter of the thousands of offices that kept the Terran Ring spinning. Every aspect on Terra— food, water, health, safety, security, economy, education, justice, diplomacy—everything was decided here. Keeping a metal ring that weighed as much as a decent fraction of the Moon in orbit around the Earth, while its massive sections themselves spun transversely for artificial gravity, with five billion passengers aboard, required a bit of maintenance from time to time. The Archonate did nothing else.

Sadhana was in her early sixties, a very pleasant looking woman with long dark hair streaked with grey. She wore it in a bun, under a silk sari used as a veil and then tucked around as a shoulder scarf. Her round eyes were both black and shiny, reflecting back an ebony luster, especially when she smiled. The crow's feet around them didn't harm her appearance at all and in fact were almost comforting. Here was a grand dame that nonetheless wore such an earthy and convivial face that its authenticity had to be genuine. She was beaming now, taking a close look at the young man in charge of escorting her. They'd met before and although she disagreed with his politics, she, like almost everyone else on Terra, couldn't help but like him.

Ethan Van Ulroy, only 34, was the aide-de-camp of the Chief Archon himself, Dante Michelson. He possessed a sharp mind, a quick wit, and offered sage advice unusual for a man his age. His high position was enough to mark him as the most eligible bachelor on Terra. Since he was almost too handsome and conspicuously charming, these combinations made him a heartthrob of millions, tens of millions. Sadhana half smiled pensively, contemplating the irony of two people so unalike in so many ways and yet both of them meeting at the request of the most powerful man alive. While she was short, a bit rotund, and far past her prime, he was tall, as lean and hard as dried jerky, and just entering the peak of his powers. His thick auburn hair was combed to the side and was flawlessly coiffed. He wore a thicker leotard, one that modestly diverted attention from his admirable physique and emblazoned with just the proper amount of distinctive marks of his rank without being brassy. The real difference between them though, was that Van Ulroy, aide to the militantly hawkish Archon, was playing host to the leader of Terran's doves.

The technology of attack and defense between Terra and Borealis over the centuries reflected each cutting edge breakthrough in science. The two states had never come to blows but tension between them was the never-ending impetus for developing attacks against which there could be no defense, and barriers which would render any assault powerless. In the early days Terra worried that Luna had the "high ground," just as Earth said about Terra. What if Borealis were to send a chunk of the Moon crashing down on the Ring? This, of course, was nonsense, as all military analysts pointed out. Even Terra's archaic lasers in Settlement Times would have made short work of such primitive tactics, and now even if Borealis were to catapult the Sea of Tranquility at Terra, it would never make it over the walls. Thankfully the reverse held for Borealis. Terra's ferocious lasers couldn't actually touch Borealis, the city tucked below the lunar horizon at the North Pole, situated at a blessed angle outside the range of Terra's photonic guns. Warships though could and did patrol vast sectors of the Solar System and it would be a simple matter for a Terran man of war to take a position with a clear shot at the city. One blast at Borealis' Dome would be devastating, ending any potential war in a millisecond. Borealis worked feverishly, and with supreme secrecy, to counter this peril, and the result changed the military calculus between the two sides: defense now reigned supreme.

Borealis' Gravitonic Force Shield bent the fabric of space, forming a cupola of discontinuities in space-time. It was best visualized by imagining space itself as water on the surface of a tranquil pond, with the force field as a ripple around Borealis that held at a steady distance. Matter passing through this barrier would be so violently scrambled at the subatomic level as to cause instant disintegration. Electromagnetic waves themselves—lasers or even benign radio—would also be diffused and scattered to the extent that beamed weapons were rendered useless and radio communication impossible. Sunlight too was scattered, and that was the reason Borealis gave out publicly for the creation of the Shield. It was touted as the next great step forward in Borealis' never-ending battle to tame the Sun, even though the truth was that it neither helped nor hindered the final efficiency of the Goldilocks Array. As for the higher-energy ranges of light—from X-ray to gamma—they were absorbed into the shield itself, so a thermonuclear device detonated above it would only serve to help power it. Corridors in the shield were temporarily created as it was deftly turned on and off at selected localized coordinates so that shipments of helium-3 could be exported, and to allow in shuttles that had been scanned and deemed free of any potential threat to Borealis. Even communications had to be funneled through ever-changing millisecond long apertures in the shield, after being relayed from Gatekeeper satellites that orbited the Moon. Terra, of course, immediately realized the Shield's true purpose; they'd been working on the same technology themselves.

The Terran Ring also had a gravitonic shield, but it needed to warp the astounding volume of space around the massive Ring and an incredible amount of energy was needed to accomplish that. An area on the Ring the size of

Manhattan Island was devoted to creating and maintaining the Terran shield. It was never deployed though—as the peace party on Terra never stopped pointing out. This white elephant was the focus of a great political debate raging on Terra. First, how could such a monstrosity as this ever have been built when it sucked up more helium-3 then the Terrans could afford to feed it, especially *now* that the reserves were running very, very short? Secondly, was this not the best proof that the never-ending saber-rattling would end badly—for Terra and everyone in the Solar System? When would the simple, sane, mutually beneficial expedient of peaceful coexistence and cooperation take hold in the minds of the Terran Archonate—and if ever, would it be in time?

The hawks on Terra had good answers. The shield was a back-up, that's all, and one that most probably wouldn't ever be necessary. They quite rightly pointed out that Earth below, in the end, even in the hands of the maniacs that supposedly ran the planet, realized that they had no option but to live with what Terra dictated. What alternative had they? Even if they could, even in worst case scenarios, everyone on Earth knew what bringing down the Terran Ring would mean. For "bringing down" meant just that. Terra crashing to Earth would make the end of the dinosaurs at the K/T boundary sixty five million years ago seem like a hiccup in the planet's history. As for attacks from other quarters, the Ring was massive enough to take incredible blows from Borealis or anyone else while barely flinching. If such madness ever were to take place the shield could be deployed before any irreparable damage was done. So the Terrans built their shield—and, incredibly, never switched it on.

For the hawks, the shield meant something else though—something which churned a visceral anger in them. It was one thing to have to compromise with the 500 billion remnants of Earth's population beneath them. To have policies dictated to Terra by the insignificant mosquito bite festering on the Moon's North Pole, imperiously delivered by a couple hundred thousand of the most arrogant humans alive was quite another. There would be a reckoning in store for these overconfident egotists, and it couldn't be far on the horizon. Challenging the Terran Ring was going to turn out to be the last chapter in Borelian history. They said as much openly, and they meant it categorically.

While the shuttle whirred along smoothly the initial pleasantries faded and were replaced by an uncomfortable silence. Sadhana was not without her social graces but was actually somewhat shy. Conversation, though, rarely flagged in Van Ulroy's presence and he immediately saw to the discomfiture.

"By the way, you're absolutely right, Doctor. 1729 is quite an interesting number after all."

Sadhana's face brightened. He'd said the right thing—as usual. "I asked my amanuensis about it. Amazing story," he said.

"But that was almost two years ago," Sadhana remarked, her eyes widened by his sharp memory.

Van Ulroy smiled sheepishly. "Well, I looked again this morning." He shook his head disparagingly. "I hope it's not age creeping up. I just don't remember things like I used to," he admitted.

Sadhana had seen Van Ulroy's amanuensis a few times. She remembered asking herself what his choice implied.

There were a few ways to look at it. He'd opted for Alcibiades, the quintessential Athenian bad boy. The last time they'd met, at an award ceremony for Sadhana presided over by Dante Michelson himself, Van Ulroy had asked Alcibiades what the reference to 1729 had meant.

Alcibiades, plugged into every piece of information there ever was, and every nanosecond being apprised of all the data streaming in the present by the petabyte from every corner of the Solar System, had the resources to answer this question or any other ever conceived. Alcibiades pointed an omniscient finger and clicked open a virtual board from the early 1900's. Swrinivasa Ramanujan was lying in bed in a London hospital room. The surroundings were quite Spartan and morose. Ramanujan was a young man, just 32, but dying of tuberculosis. G.H. Hardy, the eminent British mathematician and Ramanujan's great friend, entered the room. A strained conversation ensued between the two, Hardy clearly at a loss for words seeing Ramanujan slowly expiring in front of his eyes.

"You know," Hardy said, trying to make chitchat, "I noticed the cab that brought me here was #1729. I got to thinking and strangely started brooding about the amazingly nondescript and random nature of that number. Isn't it odd that some numbers aren't interesting in the least?" One could tell Hardy was only trying to fill the silence, but Ramanujan's reply was startling. Without the slightest pause the great savant gave a surprising rebuttal.

"Not at all, Hardy. Not at all. 1729 is the lowest integer which can be expressed as the sum of two cubed numbers, two different ways: 1 cubed plus 12 cubed equals 1729 and so does 9 cubed plus 10 cubed."

The expression on the virtual Hardy's face said that he wasn't just awe-struck that his comrade could do such calculations in his head, but that he could have seen the algorithm in his mind in the first place, and all within the space of a few seconds, seemed simply beyond the capacity of any human being.

"So you see, it's quite a unique number after all," the dying Ramanujan said.

One's amanuensis said a lot about the person—as much as clothes, hair style, jewelry, or anything else. The selection was as wide as the Universe, from among every entity who ever lived, might have lived, or only existed in the mind. Some of the more popular choices were angels, elves, leprechauns, and genies. Historical figures were just as popular though. Strolling through any of the Great Concourses on the Terran Ring, for example, one might see anyone from Aristotle to Zorthian II. Terrans were particularly addicted to the use of their amanuenses and hardly ever closed them down. Psychologists proclaimed the more extreme cases a form of mental illness, and rightly so. There were many cases of people falling in love with their amanuensis, or whose best friend was virtual, or who refused to take a breath or step in life without their counsel, or who battled an amanuensis that was "out to get them." There were five billion people on the Terran Ring, but ten billion entities counting both human and virtual. Other people-watching theorists had a softer outlook and pointed out that there was nothing new in all this. People had sat around telegraph offices, or fidgeted non-stop with cell phones in previous ages; this phenomenon was no different.

And yet it *was* different. There had always been someone at the other end of the telegraph line, or ham radio receiver, or cell phone. Here was a closer mechanical bond than many humans shared with other individuals. According to many experts in ethics, this was far past the beginning of the end. No matter who preached what though, nothing could get people to turn their amanuenses off. For one thing, these one foot tall, all-knowing, 3-D marvels of cyber and holographic science—teacher, secretary, confidant, advisor—were one's personal portal into the System. For another, an amanuensis was a constant, indefatigable, infallible companion. Over time they would even come to recognize facial expressions and voice timbres, allowing them to almost read human minds and moods.

Truly alarming though was what *else* they could read about the people in the wearer's vicinity, and the dramatic changes this caused in society. An amanuensis could also scan the blood pressure, perspiration levels, and changes in voice patterns that indicated stress—or deception—of anyone within effective range. This played havoc with every aspect of human interaction in society because the great shock was that there was very little that people did that was free of deception. Every single mundane task of life was affected if one went about his business with his amanuensis on scan. The marketplace was turned upside down as shoppers would ask if the price for the goods being offered for purchase was a good one. In the past, since the dawn of civilization, shopkeepers could and would answer, "Of course!" Wearing an amanuensis and asking the same question more often than not indicated that there existed a better deal elsewhere. Uncountable lies—little and big— made up the fabric that held the workplace, the home, the government, and everything else together. Prior to amanuenses, humanity just winked at this. Now that it was proven that mankind was a species of inveterate liars, no one was taken for their word…ever…about anything. Amanuenses destroyed many, many marriages, for what husband or wife could spend their life together, each having the power to know exactly what the other *really* thought? To dare to interact in public without one's amanuensis on "block" was inconceivable. Aside from having one's veracity verified at every step, one's identity, health status, state of sexual arousal, and many other personal secrets were open to anyone with the desire to scan them. The older, bulkier models used to be worn on clips on the hips, or carried in women's bags. For many years now they had been miniaturized to such an extent that they were now worn on wrist bands like timepieces of old. Everywhere one went though—Earth, Terra, Borealis, or anywhere else under the umbrella of the System—billions of amanuenses were to be seen, either open with the avatar floating over the host's left shoulder in active mode or else at least, most assuredly, blinking red on block.

The shuttle slowed to a stop and without saying a word the security officers exited. Simultaneously a leather-faced man in his mid-forties entered. He had an Earth tan, a deep one. The dark brown brow was framed by jet black hair combed back over the shoulders and falling almost to his belt. And, just as if stepping out of a time capsule of some sort, he *was* wearing a belt, and trousers too. They were denim; as a materials specialist, Sadhana knew the antique fabric. Around his neck was clasped a silver and turquoise choker. To say this fellow was dressed "old style" was an understatement. If he had been wearing a cape he wouldn't have looked any stranger. Sadhana recognized him immediately, but then anyone would have. Nonetheless, Van Ulroy made the introductions.

Eugene Lighthorse was one of the last full-blooded Creek Indians alive. He was a prolific writer—everything from philosophy and history to anthropology and linguistics. He was known though for one audacious theory that he'd proposed that put him clearly and irretrievably outside the mainstream. His interpretations of the Pre-Mayan glyphs discovered in the Yucatan Peninsula superseded everything he'd published, and then some. Those postulations had catapulted him into the realm of one of the most famous kooks in existence.

Lighthorse had ruined quite a promising career. He studied under the very archaeologists who'd uncovered the glyphs in their youths, and who even now in old age were locked in strident academic disputes about this translation and that one. Still no one could read all the inscriptions and about the only thing agreed on by all was that they were very, very old. The glyphs had changed, nonetheless, the very foundation of human pre-history, and few doubted that they didn't contain a few bombshells. Lighthorse's hypothesis though was simply a bridge too far.

When a thorough ground-penetrating radar survey of the mounds around the Yucatan indicated that they were anything but hills, the scientific community had gone wild with enthusiasm. The pyramids were unearthed by the dozen and a treasure trove of thousands of inscriptions and codices came with them. Immediately, though, the firestorm exploded. These weren't Maya glyphs, or Zapotec, or Olmec, or anything else known. What was uncovered were the remains of a civilization far, far older, and completely unknown heretofore. Many names had been proposed for the lost people but even a common name couldn't be agreed upon. The culture was simply called "Pre-Mayan," and it was confidently dated sometime around…12,000 BC.

What was surprising about this sea change in human history was how quickly it was accepted. The Fertile Crescent lost its preeminent position as the cradle of civilization, but with hardly the same rancor as when Earth itself had been demoted in Copernicus' time. After the initial astonishment wore off everyone just seemed to shrug their collective shoulders and gave in to the idea that Earth was home to a great civilization—at about the same time as the birth of agriculture itself. Human beings were quickly becoming shockproof it seemed.

Lighthorse had spent the best part of his adult life struggling to decipher the true meaning of the glyphs. By painstakingly juxtaposing them, symbol by symbol, with later Mesoamerican script, he'd made quite a number of glottochronological breakthroughs—many of them accepted as absolutely accurate. The tenor of what the codices said though, in the main, was where his colleagues took exception—vigorous exception.

"The narrative, almost all of it, is a chronicle of our ancestors' interaction with a race of incredibly advanced visitors," Lighthorse told assemblages of Mayanists and archaeologists. Pained silence and blank stares allowed him to continue at length. Lighthorse connected the pieces of this exceedingly arcane puzzle with brilliant insights, and everything indeed did seem to fit. As the years passed though, the restrained applause dampened to smatterings of sarcastic, perfunctory clapping that only called attention to the prevailing disdainful hush with which most specialists responded. And that later was replaced by catcalls and snickers.

"Alfred Wegener, the discoverer of plate tectonics, had to overcome similar obstacles," Lighthorse told the press. "He was called everything from 'blind' to 'footloose,' labeled a 'contortionist' and a 'twister of facts'. In New York in 1928, at a major geology symposium, he was booed off the podium and almost physically set upon by delegates in the audience. In the end though, whether geologists liked it or not, the continents do in fact drift. My interpretation is the correct one and history will prove it." Lighthorse hadn't been physically assaulted by his colleagues but neither was he invited any more to seminars where anyone might have a chance to shut his mouth with a fist. Sadhana wondered what in the world he was doing...*here*?

Sadhana politely took his outstretched hand. "It's a great honor to meet you," Lighthorse said. Everyone said that to her though.

"Eugene Lighthorse is..." Van Ulroy began. She cut him off. "I'm aware of who Mr. Lighthorse is."

She didn't say it with derision—more just matter of fact. But now she gave Van Ulroy a look that he took as petulant; she meant it that way too. Her request to meet with "a representative of the Terran Archonate" concerning a subject "of great importance" and directing her to discuss the matter "with absolutely no party whatsoever" was a missive she'd never received before. That the representative turned out to be the aide-de-camp of the Chief Archon—"first among equals" of the nine men who ruled Terra—was sufficient to cause a case of rattled nerves. Seeing that Eugene Lighthorse was also involved was enough to push her beyond coy politeness and to demand some clear-cut answers.

"What's this all about, Mr. Van Ulroy?" she blurted out.

The shuttle reacted instantly to Van Ulroy's voice command, "Stop." Now Sadhana was passed rattled nerves. It was happening so quickly and unpredictably that it seemed like so many old cinematic cloak-and-dagger scenes. Countless hyper-secret conferences were supposed to have taken place on shuttles in transit between offices in the Terran Archonate. She had assumed this artifice to be a figment of the imagination of directors of film noire, and now suddenly realized she had been wrong.

Van Ulroy changed visibily, instantly. He no longer wore the charming diplomatic face of a business-like bureaucracy but now made clear he represented a deadly-serious, unlimitedly powerful entity whose self-interest would be maintained even if the Sun itself ceased shining. He now spoke to her in a far different tone; the law required it.

"As per Terran sedition and security codes, I must inform you, Dr. Ramanujan, that the information with which you are to be provided is of the utmost sensitive nature, within the confines of the highest level of classification, and may be shared with no one—in any way, shape or form." He paused for the words to sink in. Her puzzled look told him they hadn't.

"But, I've been through all this, Mr. Van Ulroy," her voice slightly piqued. "I've had the highest security clearance, for many, many years now."

Van Ulroy was shaking his head in the negative. "This is strictly 'word of mouth.' Do you understand what that means?"

Of course she couldn't understand it, since only a handful of people on Terra even knew of such a security classification.

"This matter isn't in the System; it doesn't exist. Incredible measures have been taken to accomplish that. Even any allusion or implied acknowledgment of what you're going to be told—to anyone, by any means—will be considered a breach of the oath you're going to be required to take and will carry the most severe penalties for transgression."

He paused and furrowed his brow. "Let me rephrase. It doesn't carry the most severe penalties—it *mandates* them. Before I go on I'll have to ask you for your oath again."

Sadhana Ramanujan swore again, and this time the words were even heavier and more somber. It was more humbling this time. For all her status she was being made aware that she—like any Terran—was nothing more than a cog in a giant machine. She might be a famous and brilliant gear, but a mere cog nonetheless, and one that could and *would* be disengaged and tossed away should it cause any damage.

"Well, that's always a bit unpleasant," Van Ulroy said afterwards, smiling again. "Good to put that behind us."

Sadhana declined to agree and asked flatly again, "So what's this all about?"

He motioned to Eugene Lighthorse. "Mr. Lighthorse's presence here must certainly give you some idea of the matter at hand?" It did but she indicated otherwise, slightly shrugging her shoulders and shaking her head. Van Ulroy was quite disposed to answer her now, actually rubbing his palms together anxiously.

"Well, Doctor, where to begin?" He paused for the right words. "Your input is requested on a project that is important enough to quite plausibly change the calendar. I'm guessing future historians are going to categorize every epoch from before and after this event." Sadhana could tell he hadn't fished for words; he'd obviously planned this speech. "We'd like you to simply take a look at an incredible item, and just, well...just tell us anything you can about it."

Sadhana frowned. "That doesn't really make things very clear. An item? And nothing in particular that you want determined about it? Just anything I can tell you about it, is that it?"

Van Ulroy was shaking his head in agreement. "Yes, yes...I know. This is difficult to explain."

Lighthorse helped out. "It's an artifact, Dr. Ramanujan." His voice was deep and mellifluous. He spoke slowly, enunciating perfectly. "An artifact."

"What sort of artifact?" she asked bluntly.

"From the Yucatan," Lighthorse answered just as bluntly.

In an instant everything became clear as glass, even though at the same time hardly possible.

"The Bacalar Device?! Is that what we're talking about?"

Legends and rumors about an artifact found in a pyramid under a hill near the town of Bacalar in the Yucatan had surfaced, been quashed, and resurfaced again. Sahdana, like everyone else, put the device in the same category as unicorns. It took her a while to form her next sentence. It barely qualified as a sentence.

"It exists?"

"It not only exists," Van Ulroy declared, "but it's in our possession and you'll be examining it shortly." Now he was smiling from ear to ear. "Exciting, no?"

Sadhana wasn't smiling yet. She thought carefully, for quite a while, as she composed her next question. The two men sat quietly as she formulated it.

"Yes, very exciting. However you've skipped a few steps. How did such an artifact come into our possession, from the Yucatan on Earth? And why isn't this common knowledge?"

Van Ulroy was a good judge of character and had already decided that in Dr. Ramanujan's case he would have to be more forthcoming than was his custom. He gave her part of the truth.

"It's a convoluted tale, Doctor, and I'm not sure about all the particulars myself. But it's amazing how closely the story mirrors other Mesoamerican finds in the past—the Dresden Codex, for example."

Lighthorse could see she missed the analogy so he explained. "The Dresden Codex was one of only four books left of the Maya's writings after the Spanish conquistadors finished their auto-da-fe of the 16th Century. This plucky manuscript, having survived the fires of the Inquisition, wound up under the boot of a Russian major poking around the smoldering ruins of the State Library in Dresden, Germany during the Second World War—from which it *also* escaped."

Lighthorse related the history with a seemingly expressionless objectivity, but Ramanujan nonetheless detected the pain and outrage under the monotone. He didn't offer an opinion on how it was that the collective written culture of an entire people could be consigned to the Franciscan's fires, but she heard it anyway.

"Warfare, Doctor," Van Ulroy philosophized, "it closes doors, yes, but always opens others. The Western Alliance had the device since its discovery but kept it secretly in the Mexico City State. The Great Planetary War brought such chaos that in the tumult it bounced around the planet, like the Dresden Codex had, until thankfully, it wound up safe here on the Terran Ring."

Now the doctor was even more confused. "But, the Mexico City State was…completely destroyed…"

"Oh no, Dr. Ramanujan," Van Ulroy almost chuckled at the misunderstanding. "The *Second* Planetary War, not the Third, thank goodness. Or else there'd be no device probably, would there?"

Tittering about the horrific fate of Mexico sent a quick pang of irritation through her and pushed her mind into high gear. Her next question came fast.

"But that was half a century ago, Mr. Van Ulroy. Terra has had this artifact in her possession since then, is that the case?"

"Forty years, Doctor," he corrected her, and he wasn't smiling in the least now.

Sadhana's mouth turned down. "Not very forthcoming of us, you'd agree?"

Van Ulroy didn't like that very much. "I wouldn't know about that. I wasn't even born when that decision was made," he snapped back.

Now Sadhana took a deep breath, and slowly exhaled through pursed lips. She was looking at neither man, simply thinking deeply for a moment. Then she let loose.

"Mr. Van Ulroy, you quite properly set the ground rules for me, and now I'm going to set them for you. If the Terran Archonate requires my expertise about some important matter—now I see having to do with the Bacalar Device— I'll be happy to do my civic duty. If, however, it's your intention to start things off with a pack of half-truths that quite possibly will make my job more difficult, whatever that job is, in that case I'd simply have to respectfully decline and just be on my way."

Van Ulroy was shocked; Lighthorse amused. She was sure of that because he was chuckling to himself. She went on, making the ultimatum plain.

"I'd love to examine first hand such a rare object. But we'll work openly and honestly with each other, or you'll find someone else. Is that acceptable to you?"

Van Ulroy bit his lip and nodded; not signaling yes or no, but at least acknowledging her words. "I'm not at liberty to explain how Terra acquired the device, Doctor," he admitted in a defeated tone.

"Excellent!" Sadhana exclaimed. "Now, let's see if we can keep that up, shall we?"

She put her finger up, as if to say that what came next should be marked well. "And you can tell Dante Michelson himself that I have grave misgivings involving myself in what is obviously an unparalleled cultural theft. I'm going to have to have some indication that there are plans to return the device to the people of Earth." She flashed an accusing glance in Lighthorse's direction. "I assume you, of all people, must have made the same demand?"

Lighthorse ignored her, and spoke instead to the aide-de-camp. "Mr. Van Ulroy, please?"

Van Ulroy had both hands out, gesturing for her to slow down. "Dr. Ramanujan, you don't understand…"

She interrupted. "I *don't* understand," she agreed. "This device—from 12,000 BC, in Terra's hands for forty years without breathing a whisper about its existence—and I've only just been summoned to examine in now?" Van Ulroy started to answer, but she put up her hand. "Better question, though." She pointed to Lighthorse. "I can understand why an esteemed Mesoamerican scholar is sitting here. But I'm a materials physicist. How in the world could I shed any light?"

As soon as she posed the question, she answered it for herself. "It can't be that you want me to tell you what it's made of, could it? I'd have sent an intern if that were the case."

Van Ulroy now delivered a punch of his own.

"We know what it's made of, Doctor. What we'd like for you to tell us is how that's possible." He waited for the words to register properly. "Is that forthcoming enough? It's made of a material that…well…simply can't exist." He paused, he had to for something so important. "It's transuranian." He paused again. "It's transuranian, and somehow stable. It's made of element…number 142." The three sat wordlessly while Sadhana was allowed to absorb the blow.

Van Ulroy graciously gave her something prosaic to focus on, having just been struck with this incomparable thunderbolt. "It's very, very heavy."

"My God," she said in a whisper, "number 142, I guess it would be."

Uranium is the heaviest element, #92—ninety two protons within the nucleus of each atom, with 92 electrons orbiting in shells. Even as early as the 20th Century, though, physicists had played demigod with the laws of nature, creating heavier and heavier elements: californium, einsteinium, fermium, etc. Even at present, the heaviest element ever cooked up in the laboratory was the unnamed element #132, and unnamed for good reason maybe since its half life is something less than a trillionth of a second. Nature abhors all these synthetic creations, and they are all radioactive and degrade quickly.

"It's stable? A nucleus that big, and stable?" She was still whispering.

"Absolutely stable, obviously. It's ancient. Looks like shiny purple iron," Van Ulroy said.

Sadhana quietly listened to the rest of her briefing in mostly stunned silence. She tried to listen carefully but a hundred divergent thoughts raced across her mind. One that soon crowded to the front concerned the unusual progress that had been made in the production of heavier and heavier transuranian elements. The first ever produced was in 1940, at the dawn of the nuclear age. By the turn of the next century a dozen or so had been created—from 93 to 105. It had been slow going since then though, but with a sudden flurry of six having been fused in the last twenty years alone—numbers 127 to 132. She saw good reason now for the string of recent successes, and tried to imagine the sort of painstaking disassembly, examination and reverse-engineering which must have garnered this and who knows whatever other great leaps forward.

She turned to Lighthorse and asked a very simple question.

"This device—what in the world is it?"

Lighthorse was wearing the look of satisfaction. Armies of scientists had either scoffed at or ignored his clarion call for years. Now he had the breathless and undivided attention of the most esteemed scientist on Terra—or anywhere else probably. This was the last laugh for which he'd waited so long; he didn't mask his relish in the least.

"I'm afraid that if I'm constrained to answer that question within the restricted limits of 'the world' I'd be at a loss for an explanation. The short answer is that I don't know for sure, no one does. My best guess though is that it's a weapon, or more specifically, some component of a weapons system."

Sadhana's expression said absolutely nothing. She just sat quietly taking in the words.

"As I've been saying for many long years, Doctor, and as the codices discovered with the device strongly support, the Pre-Mayans played host to a race of visitors about which not much in the inscriptions goes by without referencing again and again a great war between the stars."

"Codices? It comes with an owners' manual?"

Lighthorse laughed. "Well, not quite."

Van Ulroy gave Lighthorse a cautionary glance; she noticed it out of the corner of her eye. Lighthorse was involved in the project to aid Ramanujan's thrusts and parries as she'd crack her head on this enigma. Maybe working together they'd be able to use the ancient clues and the physicist's razor sharp expertise to force some headway. The device was the seed around which the greatest single project in the history of mankind had grown. After making some good progress in the beginning, the mammoth—yet secret—undertaking had languished at a dead-end for some time.

"I don't want to put any thoughts in your head, Dr. Ramanujan. I'd rather you examine the device for yourself, read what's been gleaned about it already, and then we can speak about it."

Now all the science was eclipsed by the pure human emotion that flooded out of her overwhelmed mind, into her breast, and out through her vocal chords.

"Where were they from?" She asked the question plaintively, almost in a child's voice.

Lighthorse answered soothingly, in the voice he used for interviews—calm, deep, self-assured, a contrived cadence too unique to be natural. "There are certain places in the sky that we might talk about later, Doctor. Right now, just best to say that we think the civilization that built the device calls or called the extreme far side of the galaxy home. To be located any further away from them would necessitate leaving the Milky Way."

Van Ulroy, seeing Sadhana rendered speechless beyond simple queries, chose the moment to drive home the State's now clearly seen appropriate reprimand for her lapse in confidence in the Terran Archonate. "I'll consider the request you just made for me to relay to the Chief Archon retracted, yes, Doctor?"

The idea of the Archonate letting loose of the most important find in the history of the human race was positively ludicrous—and beyond that; it was insane. But to hand it back to Earth—that roiling, unstable, suicidal confederation of fratricidal nihilists—well there was no adjective for that. Entropy would decrease, light speed would be superseded, time would run backward, before that happened.

"Yes, of course," she answered in a humbled voice. "Thank you for ignoring it. I had no idea…"

"I understand, Doctor." Van Ulroy breathed a sigh of relief. "Trust that I do."

Ethan Van Ulroy had good reason to take comfort in Sadhana's now conciliatory tone. He was banking his career on her. It had taken some doing on his part to convince the Archonate to bring her in on the project, and he had a number of rivals that would be more than pleased if she were to bring herself, and Van Ulroy, to grief. Van Ulroy knew, of course, that on the whole this open-minded, plain-spoken, advocate of fair play and peaceful coexistence possessed all the foibles which made her more enemy than friend of the Archonate. Deep down he knew though that Sadhana Ramanujan was a loyal and trustworthy citizen of Terra. He knew she loved the Terran Ring and everything it stood for, blemishes and all. He'd said as much, repeatedly, in the heated debates that had raged, with the hawks excoriating her in secret councils, prophesying disaster if such a soft-hearted fifth columnist such as her were to be trusted. He'd only have to see to the realpolitiks himself, and treat her with honesty, respect and fair collegiality. That was his plan anyway. There was some risk but one thing was certain. He'd hitched his wagon to a star that was the most brilliant genius of the Solar System.

That was a gamble worth taking.

Chapter Five

Woe to the Vanquished

The transit from the Terran Ring to the Asteroid Belt was an uneventful but tense journey. Rittener had set the deadly serious tone. Yeshenko's venomous complaints, after being released from the brig, fell on deaf ears. No crewman wanted any part of it and quickly found another duty station that immediately required his attention. *Peerless* hurtled past the orbit of Mars in radio silence, ignoring hails from only a couple of stray ships they crossed in this lonely quadrant of space. There was some sense in the trajectory the Archonate chose which gave the spy net on Mars a wide berth, foregoing to avail the ship of the gravity boost the planet might have provided. Rittener had to assume the Asteroid Belt knew he was coming though. If he should somehow arrive unexpectedly that would be so much the better. As the first few chunks of debris swept past the *Peerless* when she entered the fringes of the Belt, Rittener ordered the crew into combat status. Only three slept at a time, six hours off, eighteen hours on. G-suits were worn all 24 hours, even to bed. The ship's fusion reactor was on and hot, braking the Peerless, sending out a furious plume of effluvium in front of her, composed of the disintegrated remains of appropriate-sized chunks of flotsam she had picked up along the way.

At morning second bell Rittener wolfed down two protein squares in the galley and made for the bridge. The *Peerless* would be entering the approach to Valerian-3 shortly. In his left hand he had some spare protein squares, in his right he carried a sleep casquette. The helmet blocked sound and light to the point of sensory deprivation depending on the setting. With all the exigencies which soon were to present themselves he'd be catching a few winks here and there at the captain's swivel from here on in. He caught sight of himself in one of the monitors as he trudged down the corridor. He looked his age today, favoring his right biosynthetic foot a little which acted up from time to time depending on the gravity. The reduced sleep made him look tired. "You look like hell," he said to himself. All the other important thoughts vying for the front of his mind disappeared and he laughed out loud at his image. For a moment he paused and wondered what Ensign Gutierrez thought of his looks, or any woman for that matter. He put the thought aside and said it again. "You look like hell." Truthfully though, two-toned eyes, scars and slight limp notwithstanding, Clinton Rittener had always been a handsome man. He still was.

Peerless was already decelerating and had been doing so for a while now, having long since passed the half-way point between Terra and Valerian-3. Slight adjustments now would guide the ship's elliptical path around the Sun into a cotangential orbit with the asteroid. Rittener buckled himself into the captain's swivel on the bridge, gauging the angles closing between the two orbits. A glance at the Near Bow Console—showing everything in front of the ship out to

1,000 kilometers—indicated almost nothing. The intermediate console was starting to show some debris. The Far Console though, which scanned out from 50,000 to 500,000 km, made it clear that the ship was definitely advancing into the thick of the Belt.

Rittener sat mostly silently watching space hurtle past on the screens for close to half an hour, only querying the ship's amanuensis to decide how much velocity to squander, and how subtle maneuvers would affect the direction from which Peerless should make her final approaches to Valerian-3.

"Lt. Andrews, make your speed…" Rittener never finished giving the order.

A horrifying alarm sounded in every quarter of the ship. It was accompanied with the simultaneous locking of every hatch on board. No crewman had ever heard this alarm before; few crews ever heard it twice. Rittener reacted instantly, screaming a pre-programmed protocol at the ship's amanuensis, "Evasive critical!"

Peerless' amanuensis hadn't waited for the captain's voice command. It had already judged the situation hyper-critical; Rittener had only called out the words in a moment of understandable human nervousness. A nanosecond later the ship's fusion reactor exploded into action. The autopilot used that power to throw the ship into an unbearable, hairpin, corkscrew course that slammed any crewman standing to the deck. They had a brief second or two to frantically attempt to connect their safety belts to something before everyone on board passed out. The best g-suits in existence were automatically deployed on each crewman or else death would most certainly have quickly ensued. As it was, though, even under the best circumstances, the crew wouldn't escape unscathed. Those crewmen unsecured, pinned unconscious to the deck by crushing g forces, now a half second later were squeezed against the starboard hull, subsequently slapped flattened against the deck above, then dragged along that surface toward the port hull by forces that shifted too quickly and too powerfully for human endurance. The *Peerless* though was less concerned for her human passengers; she was saving herself.

There were still ways to bring down a man of war. The never-ending *pas de deux* between offense and defense bizarrely left only the more primitive stratagems—methods used more or less by slingers in Sargon's army of Mesopotamia in the third millennium BC, or the cold-blooded, cock-sure fighter pilots of the 20th Century's World Wars. Every warship was clad in a thin outer sheet of molyserilium. It was tough, durable, and reflected laser beams better than mirrors on communications and navigation satellites. Turning a laser on *Peerless* would be an incomprehensible waste of power. Particle bursts would be just as fruitless. All ships, warships or otherwise, flew with a tightly woven magnetic shield around the hull—proof against solar storms. Military class shields were certainly capable of handling focused bursts exponentially more powerful. One could still punch *Peerless* though, physically. Nothing prevented that. One way would be to send a scattering, buckshot blast of high-velocity projectiles into her path. Another would be to detonate a tactical nuke in her vicinity. The defenders of Valerian-3 had opted for both. They'd weaponized a commercial ore cargo cannon on one of the nearby asteroids *Peerless* was passing on her starboard side. It was designed to hurl shipments of metal to the Earth system, and now had been adapted to fire thousands of chunks of titanium, just like a planetesimal-sized shotgun would.

Peerless' amanuensis could have targeted some of the largest projectiles and blasted them with her particle beam and laser. All that would have accomplished would be to turn the deadly swarm of thousands of killer projectiles into hundreds of thousands of molten globs that would have burned through her hull anyway when they struck. Instead the amanuensis obeyed Rittener's prescribed orders and directed the autopilot to take the random corkscrew path programmed—even though it calculated that this trajectory assured moderate damage. A stream of football-sized projectiles tore into the port side shuttle pod bay, thankfully at a very oblique angle. A few seconds later, stressed beyond tolerances, a section of the hull simply gave way and was flung by the centrifugal force into space. Everything in the shuttle bay bled into the vacuum; that included all the oxygen and nitrogen, the broken and loose implements within, and the bodies of seaman Berti Werth and chief warrant officer Findlay.

Two seconds later the tactical nuke went off. It was nestled deep within another seemingly nondescript piece of space debris on Peerless' port side, a chunk riddled with uranium to disguise the bomb's presence. Peerless should have been making toward this trap should she have taken the most appropriate evasive action. Fortunately, her random zigzag flight was taking her away from the epicenter of the blast when it exploded. The ship was protected by her radiation shield from the blistering electromagnetic fury of the blast, but was shaken like a rag doll by the concussion wave. A bit closer and her molyserilium coat at least would have been cracked. By sheer luck she careened past the ambush in one piece—but wounded, trailing gas and jetsam from the gash in her hull.

A few hours later this angry, bloodied bird of prey wheeled into cotangential orbit around the Sun, a safe distance behind Valerian-3. Her port side shuttle bay had been jettisoned. Like all warships, *Peerless* was compartmentalized, and a fresh exterior hull now presented itself where the shuttle bay had been, a second, previously interior, gleaming molyserilium laser barrier taking the place of the one blown into space. She was built to take blows like she'd received without diminishing in the least her power to continue on. The only sign of what she'd been through was the fact that she flew now with only one asymmetric shuttle bay, the one on her starboard side. The enemy had no idea what the human damage had been; there were serious casualties. Aside from Findlay and Werth, another crewman had been killed and two others, including the ship's physician, seriously injured in the evasive action.

The image on *Peerless'* communication board was more or less expected. Even so, the bald, grizzled aspect of the man, with an absurdly wild and unkempt red beard, dressed in 15th Century Scottish attire, and wearing the most bellicose expression, was enough to cause Yeshenko to mutter under his breath.

"Oh, man, what a sight!"

With only seven crewmen fit for active duty left, all able hands were strapped in on the bridge in the interior of the ship. Yeshenko was understandably furious at the death of his friend, and spoke loud enough for everyone—including the Valerian—to hear. Rittener flashed him a look that said that Yeshenko's failure still to govern his tongue might cost him more than the three days of hell he'd recently endured. When Rittener turned back to face the screen his expression was quite different. He addressed the man in purely diplomatic tones, without mentioning a word about the attack and his losses, using business-like terms that, in fact, were much more implacable than Yeshenko's derision.

"This is Clinton Rittener speaking, commander of the man of war, *Peerless*."

The ship's amenuensis had facially recognized the Valerian on the screen. It wasn't the outpost's Chief, William Byrne, it was another klansman, one Patrick Mc Taggart. His bio and vitals were being scrolled next to his image.

"Mr. Mc Taggart, whatever business the Chief is attending to, I can assure you, this matter takes precedence. Where is William Byrne?" Rittener demanded to know.

"He's dead," Mc Taggart answered in a thick brogue. "You'll be parleying with me," he said bluntly.

Rittener responded bluntly too. "I didn't come half way across the Solar System for a parley, Mc Taggart." Rittener cared very little about the obviously recent demise of the previous chief. If Byrne was dead, so were three of his crew.

"I hold a valid privateering marque from the Terran Archonate, and am here to enforce the terms of the Pallas Commercial Agreement. The boycott in which Valerian-3 is taking part has been declared illegal, and due to the strategic nature of the goods embargoed, a casus belli. Regular shipments are to resume—immediately." He paused for emphasis. "Be advised, Peerless *will* use whatever force is required to effect those orders."

101

The Valerians were a strange bunch, yet every mining outpost had its particularly peculiar culture. Living on the fringes of civilization, settlements had always attracted the defeated, the footloose, the non-conformists of society. This wasn't Terra or Borealis or even Mars. This was the frontier, the next place where humanity was remaking itself, but in serene and morose darkness, far from the heat and light of the Sun. The intrepid traveler could come upon anything in the Asteroid Belt—from purely female Amazonian settlements, to outposts run by every and any of the bizarre cults in existence, governed as democracies, fiefdoms, theocracies and anything else. Valerian-3 had been founded by Scottish refugees. They had gone back to the old ways, or rather, the "auld" ways, which explained the slang term "auldie." They themselves preferred "clansman." Mc Taggart was a quintessential, stereotypical auldie and couldn't have looked the part better had he been dreamed up in the casting department of a cinema studio.

Valerian's auldies had carved a home for themselves—literally. The founders had bored into the core of the asteroid and set it spinning on a proper axis for artificial gravity. Year by year, as Valerian grew and mined, so did the void inside Valerian, the "floor" inching ever closer to the exterior of the asteroid. Someday, and rather soon actually, the miners' industriousness would seal the fate of their home. It was being taken apart, piece by piece, and shipped to all ports-of-calls in the Solar System.

Three thousand miners hunkered within the hole they'd made in the heart of Valerian, protected from the pitiless, sunless vacuum outside by the titanium exterior shells they'd yet to have bitten into, and carefully blowing on the embers of life they'd managed to keep burning within through fusion reactors fed by helium-3. Captured icebergs and frozen volatiles which glided past from time to time provided the clansmen with the rest of their needs. Valerian was impressive as a living museum of what humans could accomplish even at these astounding distances from Sol. Every erg of energy though had gone toward establishing a bare, hard-scrabble existence. Valerian's only shield was the thinned walls of the asteroid itself, a barrier hardly sufficient to defy *Peerless'* weaponry.

Mc Taggart ignored the ultimatum and started the parley anyway. "If ye have come that far, a thought or two along the way must have been given to the fact that more than half the population here is women and bairns. Do you intend to open fire like a villainous demon, or are we to exchange a few words first?"

Rittener let out a half-exasperated sigh. "Say your piece, Mc Taggart."

The clansman explained Valerian's plight succinctly, even though at times difficult to follow owing to his use of terms from Earth's Middle Ages. Terra was putting Valerian between "the devil himself and the deep blue sea." She could barely afford the requisite helium-3 to keep the place running, much less churn out titanium for export. Cutting the price for Valerian's exports in half spelled the end—plain and simple.

"How would piling on such burdens to crush Valerian serve Terra's interests? Would the Archonate cut off its own nose to spite its face?"

Rittener listened politely. It all was true, and yet irrelevant.

"I'm not a plenipotentiary. I have no power whatsoever to conclude new treaties nor amend old ones, so I'm afraid that path is closed. Your future problems will have to take care of themselves. Right now I need to see shipments to Terra resumed—immediately." Then Rittener added in a graver tone. "And, just as importantly, I'm sure the Archonate is going to require some assurance that your embargo won't take up again as we move out of your orbit. You're going to have to satisfy me of that, Mc Taggart."

The Scotsman stared blankly from the screen, then in a bitter tone answered.

"We do nae want conflict with Terra nor anyone else. We simply wish to be left alone. It's peace we want, not war, nor anything else."

If Valerian-3 had wanted peace, Rittener thought, it should have prepared for war. That's what he told Mc Taggart and repeated it in the Latin it came in. This belated, pedantic advice got the highlander's blood up.

"Solitudinem faciunt, pacem appellant," he retorted quite unexpectedly. His lingo went a bit further back than the 15th Century. "That's what my ancestors told the Romans when they came bearing the same fiats you've just issued. You'd make an empty desert of Valerian, and then call it peace. Your peace is slavery to Terra, a peace found in graveyards, nothing more. That sort of peace can't last, and never has."

Clinton Rittener only responded with a clear warning. "You have six hours."

Mc Taggart had an undisguised mixture of hatred, dejection, defeat and—most importantly—stoic acceptance on his face. Rittener could see it clearly. Valerian-3 had no choice; it had never had any real option other than submission.

"You'll have my answer shortly," Mc Taggart said nonetheless, as if any council on Valerian could change the obvious facts.

"Six hours," Rittener repeated grimly.

By the evening watch's third bell a shipment from Valerian-3 had been fired into space. It scanned good, almost pure titanium, and on a trajectory to intersect Earth and the Terran Ring. A weight lifted from Rittener's shoulders and he now saw to a number of things that the prior emergency precluded. Near the top of the list was Seaman Third Class Abdul Ayoub's body. Muslim tradition required burial within twenty-four hours. With the crew thinned by casualties, and in such close proximity to a hostile target, no other crewmen could be spared for the ceremony. Rittener saw to it himself, enshrouding the body, saying the Arabic janazah for no one but Ayoub, and crisply saluting in front of nobody, as he jettisoned the seaman into space. It might have been a most trifling funeral, but it was all the more dignified, for Rittener upheld to the letter everything to which his dead comrade in arms was entitled, with not a soul to witness the event one way or the other.

A few hours later a second cargo capsule was jettisoned to Terra. A simple, terse message was simultaneously beamed to the *Peerless* from Valerian-3. It was just a few seconds of audio. "Valerian-3 will abide fully with all the provisions of the Pallas Commercial Agreement. Our embargo against the Terran Ring is lifted, and will not be renewed. Valerian-3 deeply regrets any prior hostilities, and will take no further part, with any other party, in any conflict against the Terran Ring." This was heartening, really the best to be hoped for. Rittener was on empty and needed sleep. He would have liked nothing more than to drag himself to his quarters and buckle himself into his bunk. As it was he gave orders to open fire immediately on anything that moved that wasn't titanium fired toward Earth and then simply donned the sleep casquette. He was out like a light, and after sleeping for a couple of blissful hours, was awakened. Ensign Gutierrez was shaking him.

"I'm really sorry, sir," she said. "But there's a level one missive from Terra for you. You'll have to take it in your quarters." *Peerless'* amanuensis couldn't deliver these encrypted messages anywhere else but in the captain's private station.

"You've been asleep two hours and ten minutes." She told him. "Nothing to report except the transmission."

Rittener threw off the grogginess as quickly as he could, rubbing his real eye and doing the math in his head. There was a 30 minute light lag between the Ring and here. Terra had only ruminated for about an hour and a half on the latest information streaming automatically back to her, that of the surrender of Valerian-3. Rittener was subtracting for the quarter of an hour required for the surrender to arrive at Terra, and another 15 minutes for the Archonate's response to reach back to Rittener's ears. As he closed the hatch which sealed him in his quarters and asked the amanuensis for his orders, he was still pondering what the swiftness meant.

"This is 'word of mouth'," the amanuensis, who ironically had no mouth, cautioned him. The amanuensis went through the standard warning routine, with Rittener responding a brusque "acknowledged" at each of the requisite junctures. Then it gave Rittener his orders.

106

"*Peerless* is to aerate Valerian-3. Care is to be taken, though, to leave the outpost intact. Destruction to the infrastructure is to be avoided as best as possible. Valerian-3 though should be rendered inhabitable. Hostile intentions on the part of Valerian-3 still present a clear and present danger to the interests of the Terran Ring, and her population is declared traitors and mutineers."

The unfeeling, inhuman, electronic messenger attempted nonetheless to assuage these bitterest of orders with a supposed empathy it couldn't begin to fathom. "The Archonate sincerely regrets such stern actions, but owing to circumstances about which *Peerless* is unaware, and in keeping the ship's safety and the completion of her mission as the two utmost important factors, such severe directives as those ordered are most definitely required."

Clinton Rittener didn't flinch or blink an eye, real or biosynthetic. "Acknowledged," he said, and not another word. When the amanuensis asked if he'd like the orders repeated he declined.

"Negative." He paused for the briefest of moments and then gave the amanuensis a curt order. "Have Seaman Yeshenko report to my quarters immediately."

Waiting for Yeshenko to arrive Rittener's thoughts turned over a great number of weighty matters, things he'd been thinking about for some time now. He set his jaw and grit his teeth, chewing the fact that three thousand Valerians had no say whatsoever in whether they were to take their next breath or not. As daunting and terrible as the task in front of him was, he made up his mind very quickly in the end. It turned out to be much easier than he had ever imagined.

Three and a half seconds after entering Rittener's quarters Yeshenko was dead, the life ripped from him even before the body hit the deck. Rittener's hands weren't up to the task of tackling *Peerless'* amanuensis, but the shoulder-fired laser he strapped on from his security cabinet was. He made straight for the bridge and melted it in three successive blasts that sent the stunned and horrified crew ducking for cover against the molten slag into which it was converted. When everything shut down save vital functions and a cool green light bathed the now vacant space where virtual consoles had been, Rittener was sure *Peerless'* amanuensis had joined Yeshenko as the second victim in this mutiny. He addressed his shocked and huddled crew quite diplomatically.

"Engage emergency back up control for all systems—all systems that can still respond anyway."

Just to let the crew know that he was still sane and had no intention of killing them most likely, he now grinned most incongruously, quite amicably even, and made a memorable quip.

"We'll be flying bare-back from here on out," he said.

Chapter Six

Citizen of Borealis

The Council Chambers of Borealis were not as one would expect. As glittering and beautiful and rich as the exterior of the city was, the original Old City was left just as it had been. The Borelian Council sat in a man-made cavern, nothing more, the rock-hewn walls left rough, the utility pipes, shafts, vents and electrical conduits unabashedly on display. The ambiance was more that of a grand meeting place of some lost Mesolithic tribe from Earth's distant Stone Age. This was the seat of the unusual democracy that ruled Borealis.

The eleven councilors were the cabinet, supreme court, and legislators of Borealis. They wielded absolute power, yet could be replaced quite easily, almost at the whim of the citizens. Politics was a never-ending affair on Borealis and most of the current councilors had been elected, dismissed, and re-elected again—many, many times. Statecraft here was like sailing a ship in the raging waters around Cape Horn at the tip of South America. More often than not a councilor was pushed back twice as far as whatever headway he could make, and sooner or later his entire ship must capsize. Only freshmen councilors could boast of never having been defeated; they hadn't served long enough.

Every 180 days every citizen on Borealis voted. It was a simple matter. Each civilian just had a brief chat with his or her amanuensis, as if one were talking to a fellow resident over coffee about the important affairs of the city. The amalgamated opinions were collated, set against an algorithm which took into account a wide range of each councilor's statistics, the current needs of the city, and then juxtaposed them with the names of potential opposition candidates of whom mention was made during the "voting." Presto, the election results were then declared—Borelian style. Such fluidity in government should have produced chaos yet it didn't. There was a core group of leaders who more or less took turns at the helm, sometimes in power when their ideas were in the ascendant with the population, sometimes out when their initiatives weren't. Terra said the place was run like a buccaneers' town, its council "part-time pirates," but Borelians wouldn't have it any other way.

Opinion rebounding so quickly and constantly infused Borelian government with fast-acting flexibility. One of the unusual effects of such a tumultuous system was that councilors were always just a few months away from going back to the status of private citizen, and so their professions were maintained. Everyone had a job on Borealis, of course, meaning that generals elected to the Council didn't surrender their commands, nor professors their tenure, nor any councilor anything else. The Council didn't have the time then, or the inclination, to sit and bang gavels. It convened regularly though to make the executive decisions that weren't already taken care of by the quite efficient bureaucracy—and did so in rapid-fire fashion. So there was no king, nor president, nor chief councilor on Borealis, but Stanislaus was the closest thing to it. He had been elected

111

and or confirmed to his seat forty-two times, while suffering defeat and losing his councillorship in twelve other sessions. When people on Earth, or Terra, or Mars or anywhere else thought about Borealis, his face was likelier than not to be one of the first images conjured.

Stanislaus came from a long line of physicians and was the Surgeon General of Borealis. His family emigrated from the Protectorate of Bohemia centuries ago when the Czech Republic was dissolved. In fact, his family—the Navrakovas—were one of the founding families. All prior Surgeon Generals had been charged with the health and safety of the citizenry. Stanislaus—on the Council for twenty one of the last twenty eight years—had expanded his bailiwick greatly. Borealis' water, he'd made clear over many years as the heart of his policy, was its most important resource. He'd taken recycling to almost ridiculous levels, refusing to allow the city to part with scant drops for even the most seemingly necessary procedures. If water were irretrievably converted, in any process which would leave it at end outside the boundaries of the potable supply, he was against it—and vociferously. That worked to his advantage every 180 days when people could say anything they liked about him to their amanuensis yet always end it with, "though he sure does look after the water, you know?" Borealis' Central System Amanuensis, "Diana," would plug in quite a bit of electoral weight behind those accumulated opinions, because as everyone knew and understood, Borelians had a primal fear of running out of water.

Stanislaus had his hands in many other places, too. His powerful voice could be heard in current reproductive laws, in the genetic engineering that was and wasn't practiced in the Garden, to promulgating sports and exercises that conformed with and yet counteracted the long-term effects of the weakened lunar gravity. He was the quintessential physician: sixty-two, fit, salt and pepper hair and beard, both the same length and neat and trimmed. He wore a smock almost everywhere, an expensive impeccably tailored medical smock, but really only an unpretentious tunic. He was never to be seen though, anywhere, ever, without his gold, Surgeon General's caduceus clasped on his collar. The flamboyant insignia was the only nod the doctor made toward ostentation and it wasn't too much to ask. Stanislaus was much more proud to be the Surgeon General of Borealis than to sit on its Council, as hard as that might be to believe.

Clinton Rittener and Stanislaus had never met but each knew quite a bit about the other before they shook hands for the first time in the councilor's private office, a rather airy but austere space directly adjacent to the Council Chamber itself. Here was the man Stanislaus had recently voted to grace with honorary Borelian citizenship. Clasping hands, Stanislaus felt immediately that he'd voted wisely.

Rittener's mutiny was the spark that ignited a firestorm of resistance to Terra's recent imperial tactics. Flotillas of "pirates" coalesced as fighting groups. These weren't freebooters, as Terran propaganda led on, but were instead a united armed militia of the many states of the Asteroid Belt. They did exact a percentage of the metals trade as tribute for protection, but even these buccaneers blushed at the staggering theft of fifty percent which Terra was trying to grab. When a few other Terran "privateers" followed orders that Rittener's conscience refused, annihilating mining colonies across the Asteroid Belt, this confederate fleet went into action. They went after the purloined shipments of metals, vaporizing every last gram of booty en route to Terra, from friend or foe, and starving Terra like no boycott ever had. Terra stuck to her guns even as Borealis weighed in. Borealis dispatched her fleet to the "disputed arena" ostensibly on a peace-keeping mission "to disengage the warring parties." Borealis' next punch she delivered with the gloves off: helium-3 shipments were suspended to all parties involved in the dispute. Borealis could not, in good conscience, provide the means for this brutal war of annihilation on humanity's frontier. That was a blow that caused energy-addicted Terra to cave in, but in a way that boded ill for the future. Terra saw every power in the Solar System, from the alliances on Earth to the combined confederation of the states of the Outer System, now buttressed by Borealis too, all ranged against her.

Stanislaus had committed to memory every glowering expression, all the subtle tones of menace that Dante Michelson had presented to the Borelian Council during the peace negotiations. "I want the *Peerless* back—immediately! Along with her crew." Michelson paused so that his next words might be weighed separately. "And we demand that Borealis surrender to Terra the stateless pirate known as Clinton Rittener." Rittener had already been tried—and convicted in absentia—and the Terran Ring only had to iron out the last little detail of putting the miscreant to death. Unfortunately, Borealis wouldn't be able to comply.

Daiyu, Borealis' Mandarin-born councilor and foreign minister, poetess laureate and honorary citizen herself, delivered the bad news. As was her custom, she spoke the simple words with the same dignity that infused her Gongfu tea ceremony conversations about art and humanity.

"Your classification of Clinton Rittener as 'stateless' is in error, Archon. He has been granted Borelian citizenship." She allowed a brief silence, long enough for her to answer the next question even before it was posed. "By spontaneous public acclamation," she declared, and with the appropriate solemnity. That was that. If Mephistopheles had shown up with a warrant for Rittener, or any other citizen, signed by Lucifer himself, the answer would be the same. No Borelian citizen had ever been surrendered, to anyone, ever, for anything, in the entire history of Borealis.

Daiyu was speaking truthfully. The citizens of Borealis went absolutely wild with admiration for this earthy European who cavalierly bet his life on the honor and nobility of Borealis. Within the lacerating scorn Borelians heaped upon anyone or anything from Earth, there were to be found hints of a strange and grudging respect nonetheless. Rittener's exploits touched an ancient familial nerve. They didn't go chatting with their amanuenses about him, they screamed it, so stridently and repeatedly that it echoed to Diana, who informed the Council. It *was* possible to ignore a spontaneous public acclamation, but it was also stupid, and rarely, rarely done. The Council affirmed it unanimously.

The Terran Ring got her ship back, along with Lt. Andrews and two other crewmen who had refused to go along with the rebellion and survived by sitting out the mutiny in *Peerless'* brig. The throw-away crew that the Terran Archonate had hand-picked for the mission to Valerian-3, with its lackluster history and predisposition for acquiescence to questionable orders, turned out to be a double-edged weapon. They had acquiesced alright, to the formidable will of their mutinous captain, who stunned everyone by revealing something no one had assumed he had: a conscience. Ensign Gutierrez and the rest of the crew who also found theirs hit an amazingly rare jackpot, and were given indefinite resident alien status on Borealis, a boon denied previously to a Prince of Wales. And now, this was Clinton Rittener's big day, the day he'd take the oath of citizenship. The gavel for Council proceeding today, by luck of the draw, fell to Stanislaus, who'd summoned Rittener to his office just minutes before the ceremony.

"Have you ever had yellow goop?"

That was the first thing Stanislaus said to him, beaming amicably and pointing to two steaming, jaundiced plates on a serving table next to a nearby settee. Before Rittener could answer Stanislaus upped the ante.

"My wife made that for you; yellow goop is her specialty. This *is* the Mc Coy." He smiled and shrugged his shoulders. "She admires you, Clinton Rittener, and made me promise." He motioned for the two of them to be seated for lunch. "Would you join me?"

Rittener didn't hesitate at an answer. "How kind of your wife. I never get home cooking."

Dr. Stanislaus wanted to make sure this all turned out right. He solicitously offered a dollop of fresh, incomparably exquisite Borelian honey. "You have to try it this way." A few scoops later and Rittener was shaking his head in grudging admission, just a little faked. "That's got an interesting taste, not bad at all." He put his head to the side and pronounced, "It tastes a little like sweet mustard."

"Exactly," Slanislaus agreed.

"Aside from the lack of home-cooked meals, everything else is well?" Stanislaus wasn't just being polite. Rittener, until he settled in and his status changed, was a guest of the Borelian government. He was being quartered in the Basement, a growing subterranean space beneath the Core and spreading under the Garden. Tourists never asked to see this section of Borealis—vast research, infrastructural, industrial, commercial and government centers were located here. The great mansions that lined the terraces weren't for rent, and buying one was next to impossible even if technically legal. Extended families lived in them for centuries and were planning to do so for centuries to come. So new arrivals, however few, were treated the same as legations, or business and trade delegates. There were no hotels on Borealis; one either lived here or was somebody the government deemed significant enough to have permitted to visit. Concerning such obviously important guests, their tab for room and board didn't figure in the least with regards to how visitors came and went on Borealis, and so everything was at the government's expense.

Rittener's quarters were spacious and well-lit by plenty of natural sunlight brought in with quite architecturally pleasing fiber optics skylights. It was vacant though, for the most part. His housing ombudsman instructed him to just ask his amanuensis for anything—anything at all—and the furnishings, artistic décor, and the rest would be subject to no limit at all save Rittener's satisfaction. His stipend of credits for food and any other incidentals far exceeded his expenses.

"Everything is well, thank you," Rittener answered.

Stanislaus was taking two scoops of goop for every one of his guest. This was, Rittener thought to himself, the best-tasting goop he'd ever sampled. It was mild enough that the sugary honey barely overwhelmed the last residual flavor.

This was pretty much savorless mush that he put down quickly enough to feign gusto.

"Best goop I've ever tasted," Rittener complimented honestly. "Please tell your wife I said so?" Stanislaus liked that of course but he didn't say so. Instead he put his spoon down, folded his hands in front of him, and got straight to the point.

"Everyone has a job on Borealis." Stanislaus said it as a matter of fact and as the slogan it was. This wasn't Earth, for goodness sake. Unemployment didn't exist on Borealis and hadn't for centuries. "So what will you do? Soldier, surveyor, gardener, miner, or something else? You've given some thought to this, no?"

Rittener didn't hesitate for an instant. "I want to pilot. If I live the rest of my days flying on Borealis I'll end up being a very happy man."

Stanislaus was rubbing his beard with his index finger. "Piloting? Well, you've set the bar quite high, even for a man like yourself." He civilly kept his opinion about Rittener's age to himself and how a piloting career, at best, would be measured into the future in months, not years. Now he stroked with his whole hand; he was thinking deeper. "Of course, I do have a thing or two to say about sports on Borealis." Then he added politely, "I saw you fly; you're an exceptional pilot." Rittener knew he was mediocre compared to the talent on Borealis but it was in his interest to play along too.

Stanislaus and the poetess Daiyu were the moderates on the Council. They worked together, voted together, and were courted by the other coalitions wishing to acquire the all-important six vote majority. "Daiyu and I have spoken about you. I'm sure a place could be found for you in the diplomatic corps as well." Daiyu was in charge of Borealis' foreign ministry, and from the conspiratorial tone Stanislaus was using, it was being made clear that "pilot" and "agent" were very close to synonymous on Borealis. The councilor's next remark took on a chummy air. "That's quite an offer to consider, Mr. Rittener. An assistant attaché is a high station, and doesn't come without quite generous credits."

Rittener hadn't come to Borealis for the credits. And the offer of Borelian diplomatic credentials, something that meant nothing less than entry into the most rarified heights in existence, even this wasn't it either. Rittener's expression of mild interest in both Stanislaus judged sincere, as incomprehensible as that was, and that made him a bit nervous. He regretted offering both like that now but it was his policy to just say things plainly. Humility wasn't a Borelian virtue and its councilors ate goop, not humble pie. He bit down on his lower lip, squirmed a little in his chair, and then slowly came out with it.

"Or, maybe, Mr. Rittener," he paused. "Maybe you're just a genuine friend of Borealis. Maybe you're one of the last people in the Solar System that aren't just bought and sold. Maybe you're here of your own volition, nothing ulterior, simply because…well…what do you pilots call it?"

"Living correctly," Rittener repeated the pilot code.

Rittener's expression had changed; it was perceptible.

"That's right," Stanislaus continued, "maybe you're here because you think it's the right thing to do. And if that's the case, with your history on Mars, the Asteroid Belt, and the rest of the Outer, not to mention your connections on the Terran Ring and with the alliances on Earth, I'm guessing what you'd be able to share might be worth an entire diplomatic career."

That sounded weighty enough so he thinned it out with a joke. "Who knows? I'm a fair man. I might vote to credential *and* retire you on the same day."

Rittener smiled at the silliness. "Hired and retired on the same day? Is that legal?"

Stanislaus smiled back. "It would require some wrangling…but yes, I guess it is." Rittener knew he was going to say it. "Everything, you know, is possible on the Moon." He almost guessed the next words too. "Your opinions, especially, about the Terran Ring are of particular importance to us."

Stanislaus had imagined he was in charge of this conversation. Rittener leaned forward now and let him know he wasn't. It struck like a punch, immediately disabusing Stanislaus of the error in his appraisal.

"Councilor, I *am* here as a friend of Borealis. And as a friend I'm telling you that your worst enemy now is yourselves. Borealis can't win a war with Terra—the idea itself is ludicrous. It simply can't be done. I know what they're capable of and how strong the hawks on the Ring are now. You're playing right into their hands with all your provocations."

It took little to enflame the strained relations between the competing interests from Earth to the fledgling outposts in the Outer as far out as Titan. Nothing was better at fueling fires than helium-3. It *was* running out and the great powers were maneuvering to pounce on what was left of it. Borealis' policy was the only sane course—and it was defended by everyone else, except for the thick-skulled, warmongering, jingoists on the Terran Ring. Borealis had always played honestly by posting the correct figures of what was mined and shipped. She'd also revealed in every interplanetary forum the evidence Borealis' explorers had meticulously compiled explaining the disappointingly finite supply left. Were the Terrans simply blind—or did their thinly-veiled threats imply other disabilities?

Borealis' original finds, tapped from the polar fields around the city, were at first heartening. If helium-3 was this rich in regolith that had soaked up such oblique sunlight, prospectors were rubbing their hands together at what they expected to find as they moved south toward the lunar equator. Things hadn't turned out that way though, and everyone in the Solar System had better get used to the fact—and quickly, as far as Borealis were concerned. There were fresh supplies soon to be at hand, around the equator and further south into the temperate zone of the southern hemisphere. But, as Borealis had said so often, there was none to be found in a vast area cupping the Lunar South Pole, extending up to the 65th parallel. This helium-3 wasteland was real. Borealis advised all those from Earth to Titan still wearing tinfoil hats about this to take them off and to start thinking constructively.

Privately Borelians were even more animated. They regarded the Terrans as the most thankless and insulting people alive. Borealis had powered the thousands of fusion reactors on the Ring, and had done so since the time of Artemis II. Now that a crisis loomed—and yet one that could be peaceably solved if but Borealis' steady hand be trusted—the Terrans weren't replying as faithful comrades and allies. They were snarling instead, barking directives and threats that made it quite clear the Terrans didn't view them as equals at all.

The Borelian plan was going to hurt, but it was the only option available—other than war, of course. Earth, Terra, and all the smaller states were to receive a fixed share of the supply. Yes, that meant rationing, but the most renowned economists, mathematicians, engineers, planners, and logisticians alive had done their best to calculate how that burden should be shared fairly. No one was to be cut off, yet no party would be able to satisfy all of its former demands. According to the calculus, a few decades of steadily shrinking supplies were left—for all. This was the clarion call. Earth and Terra should have complained the least, so close to the giant ball of fusing hydrogen they'd almost ignored for so long. There was their future—Sol—and the plan put them on notice to either make the switch or stumble back into pre-telegraphic times.

From the Terran point of view it was argued that the distribution graphs were based far more on the armies of lobbyists and teams of deal-making legations that flooded in to help the Borelians craft their lopsided plan. As for Mars, the Asteroid Belt, and the rest of the Outer—well, the future was a little less secure for them. Further out from the Sun they'd have to solve some monumental engineering problems to get at the helium-3 on Uranus and Neptune. It looked impossible now, but it wasn't wise to bet against human ingenuity, especially when pushed into a corner.

The Terrans had their own plan: the Lunar Partition Doctrine. For their part, nothing could be more fair and equitable. There was obviously a helium-3 shortage and Terra would be more than happy to lend a hand. The Lunar Equator was proposed as a demarcation line. The Terran

Ring would see to acquiring its own helium-3, tapping the fields in the southern hemisphere. Borealis could go on mining those in the north and sell the production to the rest of the interplanetary market. There it was, plain and simple, problem solved. The plan surprised no one. Terra had always just grabbed whatever it wanted, and the heavy-handed fingerprints of the Ring were easily discernible on this proposal too. The generous accord to leave the rapidly dwindling stakes in the northern hemisphere to Borealis while they expropriated the rest was actually offered with straight faces by Terran diplomats.

When the plan was unveiled it produced snickers everywhere—except on Borealis. Borealis took it for what it was and started snarling back.

"And these proposed Terran settlements on the Moon," the Borelian ambassador said in the Forum, "from whence will they receive their water and food?"

The Terran ambassador bristled. "If you are threatening to withhold those supplies, Terra has the ability to ship them in. They would be small operations that wouldn't require that much."

All the delegates laughed at the idea of water-starved Terra exporting H_2O to the broiling lunar surface. The laughter was punctuated with cat-calls from the delegates of the Alliances on Earth, mindful of another great bone of contention. "So pilfering Earth's fresh water for yourselves isn't good enough?   Will you leave us our oceans at least, or do you have plans for that too?" The Alliances on Earth had every reason to complain bitterly. Terran ELF technology created pressure cells in the atmosphere that moved the jet streams anywhere the Ring liked. They mostly liked them at absurd heights where much of the moisture could be sucked into intake scoops the size of the base of the Great Pyramid at Giza. This had greatly expanded desertification of the planet and helped spawn the desperate wars that wracked the parched planet. The Terran Ring looked like a halo from Borealis, but from Earth it looked like a noose.

The Borealian ambassador's retort was considered a casus belli on Terra. "Well, they'd better not be *too* small. Anyone entering Borelian sovereign territory without valid documentation is subject to immediate arrest. Hopefully, you're considering logistics which includes a security force, too."

There is where matters stood—on the brink of war. Terra had sent Demetrius Sehene to participate in the recent piloting match and Borealis had pretended to welcome him. But both sides were maintaining a diplomatic pretense that hardly disguised that the adversaries were on the edge of a precipice.

The councilor came to life quickly. He didn't like Rittener's choice of words in the least.

"Provocations?! You can't be serious," he said in a loud, angry voice. "It's just the reverse." Stanislaus' face was sapped of any power for subterfuge, frowning and staring in offended disbelief.

Rittener waited for some composure to return, and then held up a fair-minded hand. "Be that as it may, it really doesn't matter which side is pushing harder. The Terran Ring has always pulled its punches with Borealis. I'm telling you—they're willing to hit you as hard as they can right now." He said the next sentence very quietly, very honestly, as amicably as he could. "Councilor, you don't have to buy me. If you're asking if I have good reasons for my beliefs about Terra's intentions, formally swearing me into your service isn't required."

Stanislaus was still stuck on the word. "Provocations?" He laughed aloud. "You mean like the provocation we offered them when we refused to hand you over to Terra?" Stanislaus' left eyebrow raised. By his exasperated expression Rittener could see quite easily that many a heated debate about just that must have raged within the Council lately.

Rittener didn't utter a sound, allowing the Councilor to nod affirmatively to his own question.

"But if you're here as a friend and you have some knowledge that poses a danger to Borealis…" Stanislaus paused trying to bring the right words out. "Then it's the request of the Council that you make us aware of it."

Rittener replied as simply as he could. "The old policy of 'inviolable Borealis'…well, Councilor, you're going to need a defense stronger than that."

That had been Borealis' great protection against powerful neighbors: her incomparable allure. Paris wasn't destroyed in the World Wars for the same reason. To obliterate Borealis, though, would be as unconscionable as burning down a hundred Parises. The Borelians had let this go to their heads though, imagining themselves bullet-proof. They were at times petulant and uncompromising and their adversaries were tired of it. "Who *does* own the Moon?" was now accompanied by another question. "Why *shouldn't* the Borelians get exactly what they deserve?" Many people on Terra were saying out loud for the first time what sort of treatment was best suited for the unspeakably arrogant Borelians.

"Mr. Rittener, I must tell you," Stanislaus was shaking his head 'no' as he spoke, "if you've come so far to advise surrender, you might just as well have stayed on Mars. I have to deal with plenty here who are entertaining the same thought."

Rittener was shaking his head 'yes' as he spoke. "I'm aware of that. Was that stunt pulled yesterday to depreciate their counsel?" That might have been too blunt. He *was* speaking to a Borelian councilor—and Nerissa *was* his niece.

"Explain yourself," Stanislaus growled.

Since it was too late to do otherwise, Rittener did. He had determined already that it was time for Borelians to experience first-hand what bare knuckles felt like. Maybe they'd come to their senses after all?

"I've trained flying virtually with Nerissa a hundred times. I've never seen her fly so clumsily and recklessly as yesterday. I have to say I was a bit embarrassed for Borealis watching such an amateurish display." He stopped for a moment and shrugged. "It might have convinced a few fence-straddlers still unsure about the faithless nature of Terrans, true. That's the wrong medicine right now."

Stanislaus had determined something of his own; that Rittener had passed into the realm of impertinence. He was sure about that, but since that never happened—ever—he wasn't quite so sure how to react. He sat there staring wordlessly.

"And how surprising that all those tangles should have involved Demetrius Sehene," Rittener added sarcastically. "He's a Terran spy, you know, don't you?" Everyone in the

Inner knew that. Having all this pointed out was the final straw though.

With that the interview was concluded. Stanislaus made that clear when he called his amanuensis' name, Hippocrates.

"Yes, Councilor?" He appeared instantly—bald, bearded, clad in a toga—with stylus and papyrus at the ready, just as if it were 400 BC.

"Ask Daiyu to schedule a meeting with Clinton Rittener, at her earliest convenience. It's about that matter we discussed."

"Immediately, Councilor." Hippocrates gently tried to remind him about some color code for the message but Stanislaus ignored the prompt. He rose and motioned Rittener to follow him. "The Council will be waiting. It's time for your oath."

As the two men strode in the gentle gravity through the stone cleaved corridor between Stanislaus' office and the Council Chambers, Rittener, out of the blue, told him the rest. Rittener had chosen to take the councilor into his deepest, personal confidence at the very last moment, when it was too late for any discussion. It was cheeky in the extreme but it was powerfully delivered, and when Stanislaus had time to think about it, taking his seat on the dais, it didn't surprise him after all. This particular *condottiero* was famous for being impossible to predict.

"Let me answer the question you were afraid to ask. Yes, I know everything—and a bit more, too."

Stanislaus detected nerves in his voice, for the first time. That assured him that Rittener was telling the truth more than anything. "I *did* come to Borealis for no reason other than to live correctly." Rittener paused. Stanislaus couldn't really make out the expression in the dimly-lit corridor, the voice sounded pained though. "And, maybe to make up for the parts of my life when I didn't live correctly."

Rittener pointed to Stanislaus' golden caduceus. It gleamed even in the low light. "Fate has put you here and now, just like me. It won't do for either of us to pretend otherwise. Think about what that insignia means to you as you listen to me speak before the Council. And then support me."

The impractical, childish part of Stanislaus told the doctor that Rittener's words, certainly unusual and strangely delivered, still meant nothing more than what tension and emotion might produce. Rittener was a man who had been escaping death regularly for many years and now had found himself safe and sound in the unassailable harbor of Borelian citizenship. Why shouldn't he be giving voice to strange, garbled utterances?

Sitting in his august councilor's chair, going over syllable by syllable what Rittener had just told him, that's what Stanislaus told himself, anyway.

Chapter Seven

Imminent Danger

It was standing room only for Clinton Rittener's swearing in ceremony. A vacant seat would have been unusual for any session of the Council, though. Borelians were keen on politics and the Council rarely sat unless under the eyes of a full house. The chamber itself wasn't that big—about the size of a freeball auditorium, and in the design of an ancient semicircular theater, the rows of seats carved in the rock itself, rising one on the other at a noticeably steep angle. The councilors sat on a raised dais against the far wall, in the center. Above the councilors, ascending a good portion of the height between them and the ceiling, stood— or rather floated—a ten-foot tall, three dimensional, holographic representation of the goddess of the Moon: Borealis' Central System Amanuensis, "Diana." She wasn't dressed in the flowing regal gowns that Hera and Athena wore, nor in the noble robes worn by queens in images stamped on coins or cut into marble. It was a rather perky Diana, a deity in her early twenties, perpetually. She wore a borderline scanty huntress' tunic, cut well above the knees and made of a material silky and still rustic, translucently diaphanous and yet opaque. The programmers had played other tricks to infuse her with convincing divine characteristics. He skin radiated a heavenly glow, her lips

130

painted in a red too rubicund for reality, her eyes the color and sheen of the finest sapphires in the Titan Consortium's mural of the Rings of Saturn. At her hip hung a quiver of arrows, and over her shoulder she wore her bow, its string passing lasciviously between her breasts and pulling her tunic tighter against her perfectly proportioned torso.

Lest the witnesses before the Council become too enthralled with the State's amanuensis, Diana's hair was modestly restrained, pulled back in a Hellenic twist into a flaxen braid that fell down her back. And, for certain, one look into Diana's face is all that was required to tell that Borealis had something other than a coquette in mind when they crafted their amanuensis. She wore the same expression the goddess in myth had shown to the hunter Orion, who had accidentally come upon the deity bathing in her sacred pool one midnight in the sylvan thickets of the woods. Diana had set the wild dogs of the forest to tear Orion limb from limb— not spending a thought on the hunter's blamelessness. She was upholding the common sense dictum that embarrassing a goddess must be the last act of any human—innocent *or* guilty. Borealis had meant to send a similar message with the look they'd given Diana, and the air desired was well conveyed. Here was a gilded city, beautiful and rich, cultured and open-minded, and unique in all of creation; that's what Diana's body said. Here was a state with the muscle to tame any inimical force in space, a people that had conquered every challenge put in their path, a power on the ascendant, young enough to be perhaps reckless with that strength, so "watch out." That's what the face said.

Diana made the formal announcement. "Councilors, next on the agenda: Clinton Rittener, taking an oath of citizenship, matter number AE 1432-C." The five hundred Borelians in attendance erupted, applauding fiercely. By the time Rittener had reached his place in the witness' platform in front of one of the podiums the crowd was on its feet. The ovation was strong enough and lasted long enough to require that Rittener bow politely to the audience behind him, and then turn to the Council. He could see, as could many nearby, that even though decorum prevented the councilors from clapping had they wanted to, one of them, Daiyu, was gently wiping away tears. It had been a long time since the last honorary citizen was sworn in—Daiyu herself—twelve years ago. Everyone understood her feelings.

The emotions that drove Rittener's supporters were much more complicated. For starters, where *did* loyalties lie with Clinton Rittener? Every time a close look was taken at him he was in the service of some different power. Everything about him was in dichotomy. He was born on Earth and fought with the Eastern Alliance, yet as a liaison of the European Union. He was both a privateer of the Terran Ring while at the same time currently a wanted fugitive of Terran power, convicted of mutiny and treason. Between all this he'd rubbed elbows with the riff-raff of Mars and the underground, lightless world of the Outer. Now here he was on Borealis, piloting, of all things, and becoming a citizen. For many Borelians this was all too much; not for others though.

The deeper truth about why Rittener should appeal to Borelians had to do with a dichotomy of their own. For as beautiful, rich, exciting and splendid as living here was, the plain fact was that a profound and abiding homesickness afflicted Borelians. After so many centuries, the people really just missed Earth. Some knew this in their heart of hearts while others felt the loss as an oblique malaise that came and went from who knows where. Blue skies, weather, rain, fog, sweat, humidity and more was missed— all the good, along with all the bad—but mostly the freedom of uncertainty was missed over everything. Rittener possessed the swashbuckling hubris that Borelians found earthy and appealing, that mixture of thinking and irrational, cowardly and brave, honorable and dastardly that humans used to make sense of the cacophony of life on Mother Earth. And, for better or worse, wasn't Clinton Rittener the best, at what he did and was? Hadn't Borealis been the harbor of the most superlative personalities in the Solar System, for centuries now? Lastly, not a few of the pilot-crazed aficionados on Borealis stuck up for him for no other reason than that. Many of them were calling out piloting slogans and catch phrases. So he got quite a reception from the live audience taking in the proceedings; many other Borelians were watching through their amanuenses.

When the applause abated Stanislaus directed him to raise his right hand and had Rittener repeat an ancient promise to uphold, protect, honor and defend Borealis, over all others, unto death. "I do swear," Rittener repeated at the end.

"Then the Council of Borealis recognizes you, Clinton Rittener, as a citizen of Borealis, from this moment forward, entitled to all the rights, privileges, and protections thereto, unto death."

Now a real ovation broke out. It was long enough that Stanislaus had to bring his gavel down a few times, notwithstanding that he didn't like doing that and tried always to refrain. Diana was attempting to move things along too, repeating to the Council, but actually addressing the onlookers. "Mr. Rittener has requested to make a citizen's oration." Indeed, there was an old-fashioned, genteel part in the ceremony, going back to Settlement Times, where the new citizen should say a few words about his feelings for his new home. The audience was hushed, and five hundred fellow citizens listened intently to what the newest should have to say. The councilors were keen to listen too, each guaranteed to hear the words through their own particular filters.

There were five "hawks" on the Council, led by two military men: the admiral of the Borelian fleet, Albrecht, and the commandant of the Security Forces, General Gellhinger. Two CEOs of the largest helium-3 concerns in existence, along with the very eccentric philosopher-artiste, Mariah, made up the rest of the voting block. Four "doves" opposed them currently. The Caretaker General of the Garden, Breonia, spoke for them, because hardly a more pleasant voice could be heard. She acted the part of everyone's green-thumbed, well-intentioned, nurturing grandmother on Borealis. The commissioner of the Goldilocks Array's workers voted with her. So did two labor representatives from the most at-risk areas on the Moon—those operators in the Field working to mine helium-3 and sunlight—and outside the protection of shields. Stanislaus and Daiyu were the tenth and eleventh councilors, the swing vote.

Rittener signaled this was going to be more than the usual citizen's declaration when he silently, slowly unbuckled his amanuensis, clicked it off, and placed it on display on the podium. This was absolutely voluntary, as it was illegal in any court, deposition or legal session of any kind in Borealis, or any other civilized place, to demand testimony "naked"—that is, scanned without wearing an amanuensis. Diana would definitely scrutinize for honesty and candidness by default. It made an impression, sending a quizzical murmur through the assemblage and changing the expression on the faces of the councilors.

"What I have to say to the Council and people of Borealis is important enough that there can be no doubt about veracity." He looked over his shoulder at his fellow citizens in attendance; he was talking to them too. "As per the first article of the first section of the Health and Safety Code," Rittener cleared his throat, quoting a law written back in the very oldest of Settlement Times, "I invoke the 'imminent danger' clause." He looked at each of the eleven members. Not one of them had really understood him. Of course his words made sense, but they were so incongruous, so unexpected. Admiral Albrecht was as puzzled as the rest and seemed on the point of words to Rittener, frowning and pulling himself straight up in his chair. "So I am requesting that the Council take my citizen's declaration as both that, and also as fulfilling my responsibility in bringing the most extreme emergency to the attention of the Council."

That certainly made things clear for the admiral, who addressed him now.

"Mr. Rittener, first, welcome to Borealis." He didn't say it like the Chamber of Commerce did; he was offended already, and deeply. "I commend your knowledge of our legal system. I'm not a lawyer but I am something of an historian, and I don't believe there is a case of anyone ever being granted Borelian citizenship and then putting it at risk within the first minute." He wanted to know though.

"Diana?" he asked.

"Never." She responded a few microseconds later. Diana had read the admiral's mind almost, from his dour expression, from the anger detected in the first syllable of the first word he uttered. She guessed correctly that the councilor was quite interested in the witness, yet not in a friendly way. She was all over Rittener, this unusual testifier sans amanuensis.

Albrecht lectured him. "Our ancestors were wise enough to put the responsibility for public safety in every citizen's hand, especially in those old days when disasters could and did strike so often. They were also sensible enough to craft the law so that it shouldn't be abused." The admiral fixed Rittener with an extremely frosty look of disapproval. "You are also aware of the risks attendant to misusing this right?"

Rittener knew that crying wolf could ultimately wind up getting one banished. But that was for repeated infractions, and the few times it had ever been used, candid histories admit, it was more akin to ostracism—for mostly political reasons.

"Yes, I am aware, Councilor," Rittener responded without emotion. "May I continue?"

Admiral Albrecht made an airy wave of his arm in Stanislaus' direction. "The Chair gives and takes permission to speak," he said plainly, completely unbiased, as if simply reading from the rules book. The admiral was a crew-cut, spit and polished, old-fashioned, military man. He didn't even look to Stanislaus but kept his icy stare on the witness. The admiral's expression said he wasn't sure what was going on but that he didn't like it already.

Stanislaus for his part didn't need to pretend. He also was unsure what Rittener was talking about, but there was the distinct possibility that he *did* have an idea of what it might

136

be. That was enough to cause the nerves to be written right across his face, making clear to everyone, including the hundreds of citizens who were silently transfixed by the unbelievably strange turn of events, that he really didn't want Rittener to say another word at all.

"What are they talking about?" a few voices could be heard to say. No one told them to quiet down because everyone in the crowd was thinking the same thing. The "Twelfth Councilor," that's what the congregations of citizens at Council meetings were called. Sometimes the atmosphere could become quite raucous, but that was patently Borelian, too. There were so few citizens on Borealis that a gathering 500 strong, if sentiments within this "twelfth member" were united, was a force unto itself, and one that even the Council didn't anger without care and concern. "Is Clinton Rittener going to give his citizen's oration or not?" other annoyed voices were asking.

"It seems to me, Clinton Rittener," Stanislaus offered, "that what you might have to say to the Council would better be heard in a closed session. I'll see that this matter is put on the agenda of the next meeting." Stanislaus said it with such evenhandedness that the finality which came with it sounded equally appropriate. Rittener's response to this seemingly fair decision, on the other hand, was unexpected and close to an open declaration of war.

"If you'd rather not accept my next comments as both my citizen's declaration *and* an official 'imminent danger' warning, then just consider it the first. But I don't intend to appear before any secret meetings of the Council, Dr. Stanislaus. What I have to say is going to be said here and now." The Surgeon General seemed to be physically knocked back by the words, and leaned in his chair. The rest of the councilors too sucked in their cheeks at the audacity.

"Then you're dismissed, Clinton Rittener."

Rittener demurred, twice more, quoting the law, emphasizing the importance of his remarks. Stanislaus stood his ground, and invited him to step away from the witness' podium—twice more.

That was supposed to be that, and it was—sort of.

The irritated grumbling that had punctuated the crowd now metastasized—and quickly. "What's going on? He's not being allowed to speak?!" The outraged queries started coming fast, furious and loudly. The pilots weren't saying anything. They were too incensed to speak, now standing and sending incredulous stares down at the councilors. Before he turned to address his fellow citizens he told Stanislaus that the die was cast, delivering the battle cry in Latin, as he had before so many other clashes. "Alea jacta est." The rest he said in his second language, in perfect New English, to the eager crowd on their feet, and pressing forward.

"Citizens of Borealis, I *do* have an imminent danger warning to convey. If the Council won't hear it, I'll deliver it to the citizenry instead." That's as far as he got when the Council—although stunned at the astonishingly rude challenge to its authority—regained its composure quickly enough.

Stanislaus took to his feet, brought the gavel down, twice, while calling out in a loud, disagreeable voice. "Mr. Rittener...Mr. Rittener...You are excused!"

Clinton turned to answer him but the words were drowned out by a quickly building roar of disapproval that swept from behind him and crashed on the councilors' dais.

Two events occurred now simultaneously. Admiral
Albrecht, beyond restraint at this point, barked an order to
the bailiffs to remove Clinton Rittener. Five rows up,
Alexandrine, an old-timer in the Field, a grizzled engineer
and helium-3 rocketeer, at almost the exact same moment
gave an emotional cry. "My nephew was at Valerian-3! By
God, he'll be allowed to give his citizen's oration!" Those
two conflicting projectiles, "Remove him!" and "He'll
speak!" crashed together in the crowd's midst, setting off a
chain reaction which rippled through the assembly. The
collective decision was made instantly, and an angry human
wave surged over the banisters and through the aisle
barricades, surrounding Rittener on all sides. The pilots who
led the assault seemed to have blood in their eyes, so
different from the look of reluctance on the faces of the
bailiffs, whose tardy reactions now put the matter in another
realm altogether. Before weapons were drawn and a full
scale riot touched off, Breonia, the grand dame of Borealis,
brought back sanity and decorum, and snuffed out the fuse.
She scolded both sides, insisting that the citizenry retreat,
demanding order, and charging the bailiffs to stand down.

Breonia's people had originally come from the
Caribbean side of Costa Rica—from its Garifuna
community—and she spoke both Spanish and New English
with a delightfully pleasing accent. "Cuando menos piensa!"
She started in Spanish, and then finished the thought in the
patois English heard in Jamaica. "Cree! My goodness, but
how quickly things often happen when you least expect
them! Stand down!"

She silently caused her orders to be obeyed, glowering at
any in attendance not ready yet to heed her lawful command,
using her baleful countenance to subdue and pacify the

unruly. While she waited for the proper comportment to be restored she gave Rittener a long, silent look, and then addressed her fellow councilors with an honest query.

"The law entitles him to speak; that's simple enough, isn't it?" That she followed with a open admission. "There's the obvious concern among some councilors here, myself included, that Mr. Rittener might be preparing to allude to something classified." She paused with her head down for a moment and then faced her peers. "I've asked myself if the time for secrecy for a few things has passed." She scrambled the old English proverb, "and if he's going to be putting the cat out of the bag, whether I should vote to let him speak anyway."

There were a number of secrets Breonia had been keeping about which she obviously had grave misgivings, and from the looks on the faces of other councilors, she wasn't the only one. While Breonia and the other councilors were ruminating about this issue in front of them, only Diana was speaking. The amanuensis had never seen anything happen like *this* before and was certain that the councilors would be thankful for the panoply of information she was graphing out for them on her giant holographic console, whilst quoting the pertinent statutes concerning classified information.

"Shut up, Diana," Breonia said calmly, and then turned to Rittener.

"You have information about a matter that poses an imminent danger to Borealis, young man?" she asked Rittener plainly.

"I do," he answered just as plainly.

"Very well, I vote to allow him to speak, and demand a vote all around." There it was; as simple as that.

As the councilors deliberated and voted, Rittener caught sight of Nerissa. She had attended too, after all, with the other pilots. She was avoiding his eyes he thought at first, but that wasn't the case, he could see now. He realized she was staring at someone in particular with that downcast look. She was frowning at her uncle who had just voted—"no." How odd, he thought, that she should have the power to capture his attention at such a moment, and much more strange that it should please him too.

It was six to five—to *allow* Rittener to speak. Three of the hawks were so enraged and disgusted by the vote that they decamped en masse. That changed little though. Clinton Rittener gave his citizen's oration, and invoked the safety clause—at the same time for the remainder of the Borelian Council, his fellow citizens in open session, the rest of the city via their amanuenses, and out into space and most importantly to the Terran Ring, by spies too stunned at the ease by which the news came.

Nerissa was listening intently too.

It is unknown from whence it came or how many eons it drifted in proximity to Sol's environs in the somewhat boring outskirts of one of the spiral arms of the Milky Way. After many thousands of years of coasting and silently listening a signal was finally perceived, a signal and reception for which it was built: the first radio transmissions ever propagated by humanity. How it propelled itself toward the system from which the radio transmissions came is also unknown for certain, although it was a means not only beyond human engineering but barely dreamed of as yet. It merged unobtrusively within the trillions of comets and frozen detritus swirling in slow motion at the absolute limits of the Sun's gravity, arriving at its destination within the Oort Cloud. It focused its beacon on the obvious source of the electromagnetic signals, the third planet from the G-type, main sequence star a light year away, and began hailing. It had been hailing non-stop for many, many years—and finally had been answered.

The "Object," as it was called by the few who knew of its existence, had been broadcasting in a medium that had only recently been discovered to exist. The detection of this medium alone was enough to set physicists back on their heels. But if it weren't enough to discover a new type of neutrino, j-neutrinos—so infinitesimally small and ethereal, yet particles so staggeringly profuse—the real shock was that no sooner was a giant j-neutrino receptor brought on line on Luna then the astoundingly powerful drumbeat was heard loud and clear, coming from the Oort Cloud. The moment was at hand, stunned researchers realized, the scene imagined for centuries now reality. It pushed the subject of j-neutrinos not only out of the spotlight but right off the stage. These newly discovered subatomic particles, whether or not part of the answers to questions about dark matter and whether the universe were closed or open, were now one thing and nothing else: the vehicle that brought the first and long-awaited extraterrestrial message to human ears.

The greatest dialogue that could ever be shared was opened—with intelligences about whom nothing was known at first. Nothing mattered, even to include the clues of highly advanced information the Object was sending, so much as the earth-shaking, history-changing fact that a real salutation had been received—from alien minds. How they reasoned, what they thought and wished to convey, where they were from, or even more basically, how they counted and whether they had four, five, six or more senses—everything had to be prised from the transmissions. They were cleverly constructed, packed with encoded information within concealed layers of data, which was interlaced and dovetailed with more obvious layers. One of the first things discovered about them was that they counted and did their math in base-11, unlike our base-10 system. The initial message made that clear in a number of ways. As with everything else nestled within the messages, the number was shouted straight out and also cleverly embedded.

The opening transmission, the original hail from the Oort Cloud, Borealis answered with a carefully measured and patterned burst of one hundred and forty four j-neutrino pulses directed at the Object. The scientists couldn't hold their breaths that long while they waited for a response; the Oort Cloud was too far away. The light-lag back and forth was two years, a duration of the greatest nail-biting and head-scratching in human history. During the long wait the message was received over and over. It was 3.35 minutes long—200.8663092 seconds long to be more exact. It was repeated again and again, with a 3.35 minute pause between rounds. The Fibonacci sequence was being beamed at the Earth system, dashed out in j-neutrino pulses—the first eleven digits of the sequence anyway—from one to eighty-nine.

One, added to itself, makes two. Two, added to the prior number—one—makes three. Three, added to the previous integer, two, in the sequence before it, makes five. So the pattern goes. The Fibonacci sequence is found everywhere in nature, from the growth pattern of plants, to the geometry of shells, to the shape of spiral galaxies—and was found to be the very first message beamed to mankind from another race of sentient beings. And so the Borelians beamed their response at the Object, the beauty incarnate of the golden ratio that separated the next digit in the series being the spiritual ideal of all structures, forms and proportions, whether cosmic or individual. Yet, there was more imbedded than just the Fibonacci sequence. Scientists discovered this by attacking the transmission from every possible angle using every possible algorithm. Human acumen was sufficient to the task of searching out basic "yardsticks" hidden in the message.

Hydrogen was the key to unlocking other clues. This simplest of elements is by far the most abundant in the universe. Hydrogen is everywhere. It's the matter being fused in the cores of stars. Hydrogen is the yin to oxygen's yang in every drop of water in every ocean on every planet and moon. Great nebulas of the gas, many times the size of the Solar System, stretch across every section of the galaxy, sending out hydrogen's natural microwave emanations, radio waves attuned to 1420 megahertz. Hydrogen's signature, across the universe, everywhere, is a pulse of electromagnetic radiation moving outward at the speed of light and with the waves cresting 1,420,405,800 times per second. Since Earth's seconds would have meant nothing to the Object's builders, Borelian scientists juxtaposed countless possible combinations—one of which was the duration of the message with the wavelength and frequency of hydrogen. The first lock on the first door was opened. At almost one and a half billion cycles per second, in 200.8663092 seconds a hydrogen "clock" would have clicked off 285,311,670,000 ticks. This wasn't as random a number as one might think at first glance. It was eleven to the eleventh power—exactly. Theoreticians were numb with delight and satisfaction. Not only was the mathematic base of the Object's creators inferred, here was independent corroboration—independent, indeed!—of one of the central "crossroads integers" in the 11th dimensional eigenvectors they insisted explained the universe at the Plank level—ten spatial directions with an eleventh temporal bearing, time itself.

Two years after Borealis beamed its response—sending one hundred and forty four j-neutrino bursts, the *next* Fibonacci number—the transmission ceased briefly, then restarted. This time the Object was broadcasting its tutorial, satisfied that it had a bona fide listener. That wasn't all. It put itself into motion, loosing its orbital mooring in the Oort Cloud and falling toward the Inner Solar System. The Sun's feeble gravitational pull at these far regions, a light year from its surface, was far too weak to be accelerating the Object to the velocity it reached. Borealis watched, close to utter disbelief, as it attained 99.999 percent of the speed of light by the time it crossed the Solar System's heliopause on its way—obviously, it seemed to flabbergasted observers— to the Moon, and Borealis. How such speed could be realized was, of course, of great interest to Borealis. The tutorial seemed to indicate a space-drive powered by quantum fluctuations in the vacuum itself. The tiny ripples in the froth of the fabric of space-time were the natural result of infinitesimal explosions of matter and antimatter virtual particles that came into being and then annihilated each other. This bizarre background of existence on the Plank level was an antique discovery—the Casimir effect, from the middle of the 20th Century. The advanced physics of the race that constructed the Object had discovered that these tiny ripples were responsible for *inertia* itself, were the means by which objects were held back. They'd learned to process eleven dimensional vectors in such a way that their crafts moved through a space rendered temporarily devoid of normal inertia. They didn't break Newton's laws of motion. They simply manipulated the first law so that their ships could cruise through a section of space which suspended the standard demands required for building up light speed.

It wasn't so easy for Clinton Rittener to tell the whole story, even stripped of details. The narration was interrupted many times. The citizens of Borealis, at first thunderstruck and rendered speechless, quickly came around with dozens of questions they called out to the Council, to Rittener, and quite understandably, to no one in particular. One of the councilors himself, the most garrulous and talkative Stephanangelo, was casting back and forth of his fellow adjudicators, wearing a puzzled, hurt and angry look. "Was I the only one not informed of this?" There was a "Stephan" and an "Angelo" already on Borealis; there were quite a number of hybrid names like his. By the looks on the other councilors' faces it was embarrassingly apparent that this gossipy, voluble Italian, a liberal today but a conservative yesterday and who knows what tomorrow, had outrageously—and illegally—been left out of the loop. No one bothered to answer him. "What about that, Diana?" Stephanangelo asked.

"Shut up, Diana," Breonia said again quite calmly.

The Borelian Council's State Amanuensis hadn't opened her virtual mouth since being ordered to shut it the first time. Diana had to ignore the face Stephanangelo made and the accompanying pained bleating; Rittener found it comical, but had politely stifled the smirk. But now the electronic palpitations that were wracking Diana—recording the details of a meeting during which the minutiae of the highest - classified esoterica was bandied about openly—gave her an aspect her programmers never imagined her using. Asked a question by one councilor and told not to answer by another, programmed to maintain state secrets as one of her primal functions, and yet posting these pernicious data entries in her banks at the same time, well, if such an entity as an amanuensis could look confused, Diana did. She wore the same expression she might have displayed as when the hero Orion caught her off guard—only this time as if he'd brought Jason and all the Argonauts with him to peek at her while exposed bathing. That *did* bring a little smirk to life, a little levity that felt like a tonic to him right now. Just as his lips turned up he glanced at Nerissa again. She wasn't looking at her uncle now, or anyone else; she was staring straight back at him. Without thinking, automatically, he shrugged a little and crinkled his brow, as if to say, "Well?"

Stanislaus was banging his gavel during *this* session of the Council, for once with gusto, with necessity. He was shouting for the boisterous assembly to return to their places, and for order to be reinstated. When the last unruly citizen was shown to his seat and decorum restored, the sole remaining hawk addressed Rittener.

There was a "Philip" on Borealis, of course. Here he was: the lantern-jawed, ruggedly handsome, sixty year-old corporate dynamo of the Borelian helium-3 market. He was labeled a hawk by most, but possessed quite an opinion of himself, one too grand to fit into any one word. When Admiral Albrecht and the others stormed out they didn't seem the least surprised that Philip not only hadn't followed

147

suit, but made it clear immediately that he'd be led around like that just as soon as water froze at noon in the Field. This councilor didn't mince words at all.

"Clinton Rittener, time is going to tell whether what you've already said is going to be sufficient to warrant your arrest. You can be assured that is being investigated as we speak. You understand that, of course, do you not?" He said it so plainly, seemingly without bearing ill will, not as a threat—even though that's exactly what it was. Rittener's nods told him that he did, so he went on. "You insisted on invoking the 'imminent danger' clause of Settlement Times codes." Philip put both hands up as if requesting aid. "I've heard nothing of the danger of which you wish to apprise the Council."

There was always a slight chance that Borealis could have pulled it off—without coming to blows with the Terran Ring. The odds now on that possibility were becoming astronomical. On the plus side, here was a relatively small target, so far away, radio silent, and broadcasting in the most arcane, hardly believable, just discovered medium. The hope was that Borealis could physically seize the Object before any other party were aware of it, or at least before any other effort could be mounted. The coup had to be attempted at least. Here was the future of the entire Solar System, the next great step for mankind, a shortcut to who knows how many centuries or millennia into the future.

"This is the property of Borealis," the hawks had declared so clearly in secret meetings, the sub rosa trysts to which Stephanangelo wasn't invited. "Borealis discovered it, hailed it, caused it to put itself en route to Borealis." Their logic seemed unassailable. Rittener decided he'd use the other side of the argument, as the doves most certainly must have brought up in those same clandestine meetings. Rittener steeled himself to finish, to broach this extremely unpleasant business, well aware that every step further was most definitely on illegal, seditious, life-changing ground. In a last moment of uncertainty and weakness he looked around himself at his newly-adopted countrymen. Of a sudden he found the strength to let go the last restraint to which self-interest had clung, and it was in the faces of the Borelians around him that he saw what braced him. Their faces merged with so many others: with the confused, scared, disbelieving faces of too many humans he'd seen from the valleys of Asia on Earth to Valerian-3 in the Asteroid Belt. An innate yet evil power, humankind's will to self destruction, had been sucking the soul out of him his entire adult life, and changing him into someone he was not intended to be. That ended today, forever, he thought to himself as he gathered his thoughts.

"You couldn't have imagined that something like this would have transpired unnoticed by others?" Rittener asked the Council.

The Borelians in attendance had stopped fiddling with their amanuenses some time back during these amazing proceedings, realizing that the Council had quietly changed the status of the meeting from open to closed. All channels out were unceremoniously blocked, it was quite clear. It was too little, too late, and too ineffective though. Five hundred Borelians were still listening, and quite intently now as they realized what the councilors' look of dismay and apprehension meant.

Philip wasn't backing water yet, at all. "To which parties are you referring?"

Rittener gave him an exasperated look. It was an excellent wager that any object, no matter the size, no matter from as far away as the Oort Cloud or the Andromeda Galaxy for that matter, which hurtled toward the Inner Solar system at the speed of light, and then braked at just as a shockingly unbelievable deceleration to invite capture, would certainly register on a data console—somewhere. As it was, the *son et lumière* of the Object had set off bells and whistles—everywhere.

Rittener took aim and squeezed, as if in a duel. He'd have to stand and accept the return fire if the shot missed the target, but at least the contest was engaged.

"The Terran fleet, on a heading to engage the Borelian squadron sent to rendezvous with the Object, I'd say is fairly good evidence that the Terran Ring qualifies as one of those parties. Would you not agree, Councilor?"

Philip was engrossed in the virtual panel he'd asked Diana to open in front of him. His eyes never left it, his fingers deftly manipulating data in what from Rittener's point of view looked like nothing but thin air. "We'll ask the questions, Mr. Rittener," Philip answered, as if he'd hardly heard what Rittener had said. He had heard though.

Without looking up he fired a shot back himself. "I'm going to have charges prepared against you, for that last comment." Now he raised up and glared straight at Rittener. "Your audacity in coming before the Council, declaring state secrets in public in this chamber..." Since sedition was a capital offense Rittener realized this was going to be a fight to the death. There were no rules in such combat so he interrupted the councilor.

"Audacious? I'm an amateur. Only experts could think to withhold news of the greatest event in history and then turn it into just another excuse for another round of yet another war." There was no fear for himself detected in his words, only disgust. "Both Borealis and Terra have behaved shamelessly, stupidly—dangerously," he accused, and then went on to explain how.

There was a peace faction on Terra that wanted to share and solve problems with Borealis, Rittener reminded the Council. There was a war party too, who wanted nothing less than the destruction of Borealis as an independent state. The cloak and dagger scenario had greatly helped bring the crisis to the point of all-out war, with two great fleets now streaking toward each other, set to collide near the orbit of Jupiter. Both sides had relied on the absurd strategy of mute silence, neither saying a word to the other, both pretending that nothing at all was happening, with the populations of both powers kept completely in the dark. Borealis, though, it was clear was desperate to claim her prize, and Terra just as determined to snatch it for herself.

"You're doing exactly what those who wish the worst for Borealis would hope you'd do," Rittener warned, "and draining the political life out of your allies on the Terran Ring with the actions you've chosen."

"Allies? On the Terran Ring?" Philip sneered. "Is that who you speak for, these allies on Terra?"

Admiral Albrecht and General Gellhinger re-entered the Council Chambers as Philip spoke. They were accompanied by an armed squadron of security guardsmen, who like always, were wearing the same expression of pure, deadly-serious business. Rittener's citizen's oration was at an end.

Albrecht spoke as he and the general took their seats. "Clinton Rittener, you are both excused and directed to appear at a closed meeting of the Borelian Council next session to be fully debriefed." He was so obviously furious that he had a hard time getting the words out without showing his anger. He glanced around at his fellow councilors who were all shaking their heads in agreement. Rittener contradicted what he'd said about secret meetings; that had only been a bluff. "Of course, Admiral."

Rittener gave a respectful nod and repeated submissively, "Of course, Admiral." He had lodged most of the points he'd wanted to make. All Borealis, all the Solar System, would be talking about the rumors of an unknown extraterrestrial Object and the impending clash between the Terran and Borelian fleets, and how both were stunningly true, how both led down two clearly marked paths, one for peace and the other for war. He'd missed though with one last important piece of news that more than anything else made sense of his "imminent danger" speech. Borealis might be challenging Terra to an all out gunfight—armed herself only with a pathetic little derringer. He would be able to apprise the Admiral and the Council about the most alarming part of his testimony behind closed doors, and hopefully, in time to make a difference. "It was a great honor to be heard by the Council," he said politely, bowing to some extent. Then, after just the slightest pause, he added, almost as an afterthought. "I do have one more request to make of the Council—a purely personal one, if I may?"

The Borelian Council, all of them, friend and foe, had had enough of Clinton Rittener. Not one of them even wanted to respond formally to any of his requests, personal or otherwise. Their collective silent stares he, strangely enough, interpreted as his leave to continue.

"Dr. Stanislaus, it would be a great honor to fly with your niece, Nerissa. As I told you before, Councilor, I came to Borealis to pilot. I have admired her, greatly, for some time. If you would convey my request, I would be very much in your debt."

It started almost immediately, though slowly—then, very quickly, it built. All the pilots and many others in the crowd were whistling, that particularly lunar, high-pitched whistle in the slightly alien air. It was another thing that pilots did that couldn't be explained exactly. The idea, though, was that the sky might be falling, but Rittener, by Diana, had kept his priorities in order. This scarred, amply repaired, over the hill mercenary from Earth was sure acting like a pilot—and on no other place in existence was such behavior respected more than Borealis. And so the chamber reverberated with their whistles.

From the gallery, even though the noise drowned out her words, he could read her lips. "I *will* fly with you, Clinton Rittener," she was saying.
And, for once, she was almost smiling.

Chapter Eight

The Pilots' Code

Their second meeting the very next morning wasn't a thing like the first.

"Well...traitor, hero, scholar, warrior, diplomat...I don't believe I've ever met anyone like that," Nerissa said, her words accompanied by a wry smile. "You're really not sure *what* you'd like to do, are you?" The mild sarcasm was more than paid for though by her next sentence. "I've never seen such a courageous case made in the Council, and I want to apologize for having misjudged you."

She held out her hand to intensify the surrealism. Clinton Rittener *was* all those things, depending on who was talking, but he was also human—and male. Nerissa had said those words to billions of men, in their fantasies. So there were any billions of daydream responses from which to choose. The plain truth was that Nerissa's open, almost flirtatious extension of friendship was something no man alive really planned for. He was as clumsy as any man would be.

"Apology accepted," he said, taking her hand. Her fingers, like her limbs, were long and sleek, the nails brushed with glitter that sparkled in the dayglow. His smile was masking his nervousness. "Maybe it's just because I can't get her out of my mind—from yesterday—but you *do* look a lot like Diana." Then he corrected himself. "All but for the eyes, of course." He moved his head as if trying to shake off the image. He laughed a little at the way the amanuensis' gaze was meant to cause everyone to cower, and she laughed with him.

She'd only awoken, Rittener could tell, and was showing him a fresh side of her that only a lover and few else might see, her hair still uncombed, braided quickly for flying. This was delicious for Rittener just as it was, sharing a flight with the preeminent pilot alive, who also could pose as the model for a sex token on one of the fetish settlements in the Asteroid Belt.

Strolling next to him, her step in graceful harmony with the lunar gravity, she stood only half an inch shorter than him, and Rittener was a very tall man. Such an imposing frame was somehow yet delicately constructed—lithe, nubile and swan-like. Nerissa's allure, her uniqueness, came from those kinds of dichotomies because she was a complex creature of diametrically opposed qualities, somehow contained within the same beautiful female animus. Her delicacy was yet another contradiction, for that was appearance alone; her stamina and will were absolutely unbounded. Nerissa used the contradictions and dualities that animated her personality to quite an effect, sufficient to take men's feet out from under them. This princess, the niece of one of the Borelian councilors, the most famous flyer alive, and most probably a former or current spy to some degree, was also this sweet-smelling, hair-tousled, coquette in front of him. Even that had its mirror image because she'd worn a particularly modest leotard, one so proper and reserved that it had to have been chosen quite purposefully. As she took his hand again she seemed shy and coy, and yet possessed of an eagerness barely hidden for dignity's sake.

"Something else I think I've had to change about you, too. You came here to fly, didn't you? You're a real pilot, aren't you, Clinton Rittener?"

This was even more personal and flattering, because pilots, well, they were a breed unto themselves.

Different colored racing charioteers, in ancient times, each led their rival factions in Rome, Alexandria, and elsewhere. They were powerful enough to almost bring down emperors. During the Nika Riots in Constantinople, Justinian had to flee from them to the city's harbor on the Bosporus to take ship, and was only turned back at the last minute by his steel-hearted, cold-blooded wife, the Empress Theodora, who told him famously that "royal purple doesn't run!" Gladiators' sweat sold for such a price that only high-born patrician maidens could afford it, and centuries later the perspiration of rival knights and chevaliers who jousted soiled the kerchiefs of swooning countesses and marchionesses. Sport had always shaped society, and society done so with sport, since the beginning. Golfers had been businessmen, and cricketers, gentlemen. It was ruffians who played by the rules they created for ice hockey and rugby, and footloose partying surfers who invented a dialect to go with theirs. Pilots, too, had their own culture and etiquette. To many it was more than that, and to some it was almost a religion.

Pilots believed in absolutes, since they faced them constantly as they flew: exhilaration, endurance, confidence, and the rest. Each of these and every other quality existed somewhere, a perfect good and bad that suffused the universe, perhaps, many pilots believed, embedded in the very fabric of the nothingness of the vacuum of space. People had known this void since Old Modern times, but in the current era, with the realm of humanity measured much less as solid ground and so much more as the vast, empty expanse of the Solar System, the effect of that sea change was seen in a thousand places, piloting but one. The piloting code was pure simplicity, but roiling at the same time with an infinity of agreements and contradictions within, just like the incomprehensible quantum froth that lay beneath the surface of nothingness itself.

Pilots just "lived correctly." If that meant lying were the path that produced the real good, a pilot would be expected to lie. If truth did more good, nothing could induce a lie then. That same simplicity ruled every other action. Everything was allowed, up to murder and beyond, while anything might be forbidden at the same time. The basic philosophy was that every sane human knew instinctively what course to take to preserve dignity, to uphold the affirmative interior view of self, in short, to live one's life as a positive rather than a negative force. Pilots didn't waste too many words describing it; the code was something that should come naturally to the flyer. Part of the shorthand was that as rare as it was for a person to venture into the public arena without an amanuensis, it really wasn't that unusual for pilots to "go naked" like that. Neither Clinton nor Nerissa were wearing theirs. It was a statement that said that deception—among many other things—was really self-deception at heart.

They boarded the piloting elevator and touched the tab to the expert level. Ascending presented yet another breath-taking panorama of wondrous Borealis.

"Where do poets promise to steal Borelian women away to? That must present a problem as a literary device—with paradise right here?" Rittener asked the question in all seriousness, quietly, staring in awe at the vista before them. Nerissa, native-born but not yet jaded with the city's beauty, was transfixed too.

"It's going to be better in a while," she answered simply.

There were no words to describe the bird's eye view of a pilot flitting around the gilded city of Borealis. Powered by one's own muscles, truly flying like Icarus, or even much older dreams—as human winged figures painted in Neolithic cave dwellings showed—well, just calling such dreamlike ecstasy "better" didn't really do, but then no words would.

When they reached the launch platform and Rittener was helping her buckle on her wings he asked her the same favor everyone did. "If you've got any advice for me, before we start…?"

She looked at him blankly. "Well, I'd have to see you fly first, Clinton Rittener." She waited for the wisecrack to sink in, hiding her smirks, and then added. "I can't see behind me when I fly." He wasn't sure if Nerissa of Borealis was flirting with him, but she certainly was joking with him, even if it was at his expense, and soon—would be flying with him. This would be a good moment to press frozen in time if such a button had existed.

"That's true," Rittener agreed. "Keep an eye on my dives, though, if you would? I'm already pretty much an expert at crashing into people." The minute he said it, he almost wanted to pull the words back, not sure if he should have referenced her tangles with Demetrius Sehene with his tongue in his cheek. But Nerissa took it good-naturedly. And, she was determined to have the last riposte.

"Diving? That comes at the home stretch." She made a gesture with her hand that suggested that was a long way down the path for Rittener.

Sitting and catching their breaths under Kepler's Arch, recuperating after the flight, they talked of many things. Not a word though passed between them about anything he'd said in the Council chambers, he too certain he'd already spoken far enough out of turn to last a lifetime on Borealis, she too polite obviously to tempt him to do more damage. There were plenty of other things of which to speak. They talked about the marvels of the Solar System they'd both been fortunate enough to see for themselves, and laughed about the strangest habits and customs of those far off places.

"Speaking of the most unusual customs, you *are* sitting under Kepler's Arch, you know." Nerissa asked him if he'd made his wish yet. The arch was the largest single piece of solid gold in existence. Anyone fortunate enough to sit underneath it could make a single wish, but only once in an entire lifetime. She interpreted by his laugh that he hadn't.

"Well, don't wait too long," she lectured him like one of the city's guides. "There are cases of people who lived their entire lives on Borealis and had died without wishing. They hadn't wanted to waste it, and waited for the perfect time that never came."

Wishes, and things that came true or didn't, and the fatigue that overtook both of them now as they sat and collected themselves—this had both of them sharing a quiet moment. She had noticed his ring, the single piece of jewelry he wore. Sitting next to him, she boldly took his hand, enticing it toward her.

"What's this?" she asked him. It was an unusual ring, on its face embossed a red salmon leaping over three blue waves. He pulled it off and handed it to her.

"Have a look at it. It's very, very old. From the beginning of the 20th Century—1914, to be exact."

Nerissa was enthralled. "I love antiquities!" The enthusiasm in her eyes was real. "This must have an amazing story. Does it?" If it hadn't Rittener would have had to make one up for her on the spot rather than disappoint her.

"A very amazing story, actually," Rittener said confidently. "One of my ancestors exchanged buttons with an English Tommie during the World Wars, the First one. That fish, and the waves, that's the insignia of the British Second Corp. It was passed down all these years, someone made a ring out of it, and here it winds up on the Moon under Kepler's Arch."

Of course, the ring and story had more than piqued her interest. She held it up to the dayglow reflecting off the Dome to get a better look at it.

"Why were they exchanging buttons?" she asked. "Was that when the war ended?"

He answered her first with a contradictory, disconcerted puff of air. "It's a sad story, Nerissa," he warned her,

161

winking his green eye a little. "You sure you want to hear it?"

The Christmas Truce on the Western Front in 1914 was more than a poignant story. It was the title page of an epic of carnage and slaughter that had been the history of bleeding Earth from then on, and *still* at it. German and English troops, dug into opposing trenches and having just undergone the most horrific six months ever experienced in warfare, of their own accord on both sides, against their officers' wishes, exhausted by the killing, just put down their weapons on Christmas Eve, 1914.

"So, they met in the no man's land between the wires, bearing gifts, exchanging cigarettes, singing holiday songs, playing soccer—and swapping insignia." Rittener was going to go on, but left it right there. It was just as well since Nerissa didn't want to hear any more.

"Oh, I don't want to know the rest," she said, closing her eyes and crinkling her nose. "They, of course, had to go back to it the next day, right? They went back to killing each other the very next day, that's how the story ends?"

She took his hand and pushed the ring back onto his finger, shaking her head in distress. "You've got a relic of a nightmare here, Clinton Rittener."

He nodded his head in agreement but had a good answer. "It was my father's. It's really one of the very few things of his that I have."

Nerissa was still holding his hand when he said that. Now she took the other one too, sitting so close to him that he could smell her damp hair and the slightly sweet scent of her perspiration on her leotard.

Her next words went straight inside him, to the deepest place. "That change in you that you spoke of in the

Council." She was looking straight into his eyes. "That made a great impression on me. This is part of that, isn't it?"

Rittener looked confused. "But I never said anything about any change that's come over me."

Nerissa lifted an eyebrow. She could see inside men, her look said. She could see inside him, at least. That's what her words said too.

"No, you didn't say that outright. But I heard everything you were saying, Clinton Rittener."

Maybe it was possible for women like her to peer within and see the wounds inside him. A change *had* built in him, growing for a long time now, and overpowering him finally at Valerian-3. It pleased him greatly to think that Nerissa could actually see it. She must have seen something, though, because a tear was welling in her eyes.

"I want you to know that we might disagree on some important things—but I'm on your side. As a Borelian, as a pilot, as a friend."

Rittener reached over and wiped the tear from her cheek. "You're not wasting a wish on me, are you?" he asked. She pushed his hand away and laughed. "Diana, you are arrogant, aren't you? Of course not, I made my wish a long, long time ago."

She squeezed his hand and said it again.

"But I'm on your side, Clinton Rittener. I swear it."

He heard her promise, under Kepler's Arch, listening to her sweet words, taking in her unadorned yet fragrant body aroma—while making a silent wish of his own.

Chapter Nine

Gotterdammerung

Like many catastrophes, this one too came without much warning. Borelians didn't see the fleet arrive with their own eyes, having scrambled en masse into the Core at the sound of the alarms. Unlike other disasters that struck other great cities in the past, there was no mad panic for one, as there had been at dawn in Los Angeles, for example, when it was leveled by the series of great earthquakes on the summer solstice of 2017. The natural impulse to run scared and flee, which had emptied countless cities before countless invaders, was missing too. That didn't mean though that morale hadn't already been struck a mortal blow. Like a last stronghold of a crusading order now surrounded on all sides by a sea of enemies, Borealis saw her stark circumstances in the same light. There was no place to escape, and Borelians thought they might actually be glimpsing the arrival of the city's end, an idea that spread like a virus.

The population of Borealis had prepared for several war scenarios with the Terran Ring. Unfortunately, none of those were unfolding. Instead, the terrified population was being treated to an unending series of strong rumbles from tremendous explosions, and most disturbingly, from *within* the shielded perimeter. Thousands of holographic replicas of Diana appeared everywhere within the Core, at the juncture of every corridor, at every public place, in the private quarters of every citizen.

"Borealis is under attack. This is not a drill. Borealis is under attack." She said the words so calmly, so incongruously as to what was being declared. "Martial law is in effect, so do your part to maintain a safe and secure Borealis. Clear all corridors immediately, and above all, remain calm. The authorities are taking measures to ensure the security of the city. Remain calm."

Diana wasn't being totally honest though. Borelian Security Forces weren't taking any measures at all but were simply riding out the disquieting jolts like everyone else, and wondering, like everyone else, what was going on. It wasn't possible for any of this to be transpiring—yet it was.

The Terran fleet, taking an outwardly spiraling orbit centered above the Lunar North Pole, was leisurely pounding every square meter of the Shadow Zone between the ridge line at the edge of the crater supporting the Goldilocks Array, to the periphery of the Garden where the lush fields terminated against the air locks and sally points. There was nothing to destroy here, thank goodness, but the massive, pulsed particle beams, meant obviously to terrorize the citizenry, packed such a horrific punch that they brought down part of the city indirectly. In the places where the Shadow Zone lessened to a thin corridor, the blasts had undermined the crater walls and brought down some of the titanic mirrors anchored above. A few had crashed straight through the dextrite ceiling between the agricultural fields and the black, airless vacuum above. Efficient emergency airlocks did their job, cauterizing the wound, but a number of sections were gone. There'd be very little cucumber, peas, and okra on Borealis this season. None of this was possible—and yet it was most assuredly happening.

"What has happened to the shield?" Frightened voices were asking this question in all the shelters. "And, where was the Borelian fleet?"

Diana wasn't addressing any of those important queries. "The authorities are doing everything in their power to take control of the situation. Please, above all, remain calm."

The Borelian Council, quite to the contrary, at that very moment, was having the last remnant of its control snatched from its grasp, and by someone who had striven for this moment with unceasing passion, the Chief Archon of the Terran Ring.

"Have our shots across your bow got your attention, Admiral?" It was Dante Michelson himself, not the commander of the Terran fleet. He was being patched through from the Ring, it was assumed anyway, because not even the pretense of the slightest diplomatic niceties was observed. That was Michelson's opening remark and it didn't bode well at all.

Dante Michelson was not blessed with a handsome appearance, and further, he'd not done the best with what nature had allotted him. His skull was thick, asymmetrical and knotty, and those unsightly characteristics were highlighted by the fact that he kept his hair trimmed so short that it possessed no style at all, just a stubble which covered the scalp, save for a wide bald patch that dominated the crown. Two thick, incongruous sideburns accentuated the fleshy jowls that made a naturally rectangular face seem far too square to please any eye.

Michelson, hardly an Adonis, had nonetheless acquired the lordly habits of the extreme upper crust of humanity, his gestures, expressions, and very countenance appropriate for a grandee of the 16th Century. He was no patrician, though. He'd been a merchant, like his father and grandfather— groceries, cosmetics and other sundries—a fact he felt ill at ease discussing and might even have forgotten, if one judged by the terms he used for "low tradesmen," himself somehow but certainly not included.

Simply put, he had the face and bearing of an unattractive, airy, upper-crust bully, and that would have said it all, except for the stunning aspect of his eyes. They were nothing less than intimidating; two giant, ebony pools that demanded the attention of anyone upon which he cast his gaze, a look part praying mantis, part raptor, and which exuded a dangerous intelligence. For better or worse, one way or the other, by the sheer force of unlimited will, this grocer's son had become the most powerful man alive. In his company it was the rare individual who didn't keep that fact in the very front of the mind.

Admiral Albrecht couldn't answer him, his lips trembling with frustration but sealed tight by the force of sheer shock. Breonia, who also was seething, responded for him.

"Even Genghis Khan declared war, Mr. Michelson." She said it in as ugly a way as the words implied. "Is the Terran Ring, sir, at war with Borealis?"

Michelson forced a fake laugh, the kind made by people not very practiced in the real ones. "War is declared by one state to another," he lectured. "You've obviously not been listening to us for the last few decades, have you? We're not here to declare war, but to put an end to a rebellion, one that's gone on for long enough."

Before she could answer Michelson had his hand up. It was his way of signaling that this *was* the beginning of the end.

"There is to be no discussion about matters already endlessly debated. No negotiations are requested, nor will they be entertained or tolerated. I'm here to deliver the terms of your surrender." He paused, and in an odd tone of almost friendly conviviality, as if allowing the councilors into his confidence when he certainly need not, the archon let them in on something. "The fact that there *are* terms, that we *are* talking, says volumes about the amazing restraint Terra shows, and the reluctance to bring more force to bear on Borealis than is necessary." In case the councilors didn't understand he said it right out for them. "There are some on Terra that wouldn't have the Archonate offering any terms at all. So I strongly suggest that you consider wisely the articles of the accord we're sending along."

Breonia ignored the diktat and asked what Admiral Albrecht was too angry and distraught to put into words. "This Terran reluctance to bring force to bear, does that explain the disappearance of half the Borelian home fleet?"

The Borelian fleet hadn't disappeared actually. Those ships which happened to be in lunar orbit on the Earthward side when the attack began were being scanned as millions of pieces of flotsam circling the Moon. Their shields also, for reasons completely unexplained, had failed too. Michelson was disposed to explain that and put the brightest spin he could on the annihilation.

"Those Borelian warships that made clear that their intentions were to exit the battle were allowed to withdraw from the field." That was the diplomatic way to detail that Terra had destroyed half of the Borelian home fleet with all hands lost, and scattered the rest into space, in all directions outward. Michelson gave the impression that it was Terra's largesse and humanity that accounted for the difference between the disaster at hand and the unmitigated catastrophe that could have been. The truth is that neither he nor anyone else was sure about the effective distance of the new technology which was operating so superbly, creating "wormholes" in Borelian shields, and keeping them open long enough for pulses of death-dealing particle beams to vaporize warships, or to pound the lunar surface along Borealis' Shadow Zone. The eleven-dimensional magic which tipped the balance so completely in Terra's favor was being generated on the Terran Ring itself and the infrastructure which powered it couldn't be fit into a Valerian sized asteroid, much less a Terran warship. But it was in Terra's interest to let Borealis wonder if her expeditionary fleet, closing in on both the Object and approaching Terran war ships near Jupiter orbit, might not also be heading for an equally calamitous tragedy as the home fleet had just suffered.

The *Art of War,* from China, from Earth's ancient past, said that it was the supreme craft of any general to subdue the enemy without a fight. Michelson, paying homage to that dictum, was leaving the Council in power just long enough to order her fleet to internment at Terra, their last act—before surrendering the city. There was a new reality to acknowledge and it was starting right now, the archon's tone and glower said distinctly.

"The facts are quite simple," Michelson concluded with the silent, cowed councilors, "resistance or hostilities, here or anywhere else, will be met with severe and immediate consequences in Borealis." He made the threat and demand as plain as glass. The former ambassador, who'd been forced to sign a humbling agreement by these same Borelians, was back now—to tear up the accord.

There was to be a very different Borealis, indeed.

The arriving tram's doorways opened to debouch a silent, somber party. They walked briskly, all business, their synchronized military boot steps clicking on the polished metal floor of the corridor. Rittener, accompanied by a detail of heavily-armed, expressionless Security guardsmen, knew he must be mere yards from the exact lunar North Pole but didn't ask anything about it. He was more surprised and interested in the activity all around him; the bustle said that the maglev was still in operation, in a city completely locked down under martial law. Borealis' accelerator, built precisely at the pole to give the widest possible targeting range, shunted helium-3 to all parts of the Solar System. Unlike the old-fashioned cannons that explosively fired canisters to Earth and the Terran Ring, Emma—electro-magnetic materials accelerator—used a wave of powerful magnetic pulses, pushing from behind, pulling from ahead, to reach escape velocity.

A last security lock slid open at the voice command of the subaltern escorting Rittener, to reveal a truly unexpected scene. Rittener at first had no idea what it all meant. Emma's control room was a beehive. Two councilors— Stanislaus and Breonia—along with their staffs and a military contingent at their step, all crowded in with the engineers and stevedores who operated the maglev. His eye then went to Nerissa and he realized in an instant what everything meant, and he could feel his heart sink. As their eyes met, though, he quickly found the strength to reach inside and right himself. He gave her a rakish smile, more for himself than for her, strode right up to Stanislaus and in the age-old tradition of fighter pilots, rodeo riders, gunslingers, gladiators and all the others who never lost their nerve—joked.

"Am I under arrest, Councilor?"

Stanislaus' defeated, rest-deprived look told Rittener that the councilor was almost sleepwalking through a nightmare from which he wasn't going to wake. It was too late for the debriefing, too late to discuss the solid intelligence that spooks and agents out to Titan had been whispering about lately—a new Terran weapon which could, astonishingly, pierce shields. It was too late to extend a hand to the faction on Terra that wanted peace, who were themselves kept in the dark about most of what Terra did and didn't do. All that was left was for Rittener to end this the right way, courageously if he could.

Stanislaus responded with some gallows humor of his own. "I'm afraid it's worse than that. We've found a job for you, after all—a commission in the Service." Rittener thought for a second about which fate was more dangerous and silently cursed his luck.

With his right hand up and repeating the words, he couldn't help but be distracted by the mega-magnets operating so near, switching on and off in their billionths of a second, behind and in front of cartridges that hurtled down the electromagnetic sled. Emma made an uncomfortable, scary sound, a "swoosh" that came from the walls around

172

them, rather than the airless, soundless barrel firing projectiles at escape velocity and higher.

Not that it probably mattered that much, but Rittener had to ask anyway. "What's my rank?"

"Commander," Stanislaus said.

Rittener frowned a little; that really wasn't that high. He made use of the frown, as long as it was there, nodding his head in the direction of the breech of the giant accelerator.

"Is one of those cargo canisters going to be my first command?"

Nerissa now had tears in her eyes. He could see them welling up the minute he entered Emma's control chamber, and now they were streaming down her face. No one could cry like Borelian women, the tears so plump and languid, the fragile gravity caressing the droplets. She was wearing a *dress*—so old-fashioned, so feminine, so girlish, and crying just like that. But her hair, well, it was unbraided, cascading freely off her cheeks and flowing past her shoulders, with the strands pushed away from her face, damp with salty tears. It was more than he, or any other man, could honestly be expected to resist, even with the sound of Emma punching the heavens with kilometer per second blows dominating the background.

"You have the most beautiful hair I've ever seen in my life," he said, stupidly, humanly, honestly—mostly realizing that he'd probably never be able to say that if not now. He had more to tell her, but it caught in his throat. And she'd stepped to him anyway, taken his hands—both of them, the way Borelians do with close friends—and was doing all the speaking.

"They specifically asked for you. Turning you over to them is on the list of demands they've made." She stumbled

173

through the words, realizing she was repeating Rittener's death warrant to him. Then she wiped her cheek and put on a braver face. "You're to join our fleet in the field. You're going to be part of Borealis' last chance, Clinton." It was the first time, he realized, that she'd ever called him by just his Christian name.

Breonia had been taking everything in wordlessly. She now shared some advice with Rittener, her grand-maternal bearing quite alive and well, only now showing the kind of teeth an experienced, old lioness bares.

"You should know Borealis has nothing to gain or lose with Terra in handing you over, or in sending you off to the center of the galaxy, either one. They've made it clear; they're taking everything." She paused and then repeated for emphasis. "Everything."

It wasn't just for pure spite either that Borealis was giving Rittener this dangerously unlikely glimmer of the hope of escape. "But there is that too," Breonia admitted to Rittener, almost cursing Terra under her breath.

"Mostly, come een like, you're only getting in this poppy show because this young lady begged her uncle, and her godmother too, for your life."

Stanislaus thought Rittener understood her, so he added his piece, too. "You're going to have to beat big odds, Commander, for even the possibility of following these orders. The Borelian fleet's last directive is to scatter, to save itself, to survive, to live long enough to fight another day." He pointed to Emma. "You have to realize your chances are terrible, yes?"

"Cha! Cho!" Breonia scolded Stanislaus. "*Valga me, Dios!* What are you scaring him for? The young man will be alright, or else how will he come back for her?" She

174

looked at Rittener and stunned no one by winking at him. That worked for her, a lot. Her aquiline, *mestizo* nose, perfectly shaped and noble-looking in an antique way, sat between two aged yet clear eyes that said they had seen everything. Those winks, at the epicenter of deep smile lines, indicated that the lady possessed ancient knowledge and was happiest when she could share it with her fellows.

"I don't suspect patriotism will cause you to scour the Solar System, finding a way to oppose Terra and rescue Borealis' fortunes." She gave a tender, familial look in Nerissa's direction. "But I don't doubt that something will bring you back here, and that such a day dawns soon, I pray."

Nerissa had been squeezing Rittener's hands, not letting go. Just as Breonia finished, another cargo canister was flung off the Moon at a terrifying speed, announcing a new, now pressing foreshadow of the impending trial at hand. The noise scared Nerissa, enough to cause her to pull Rittener close and whisper against his cheek. "Don't die, Clinton," she said with her eyes wet and half-closed. And then in a voice louder, for everyone to hear, still embracing him tightly, she told him what he had first told her.

"Good flying, Clinton," she said bravely, but really, half-heartedly.

Rittener brushed her hair to the side, barely daring to touch, and promised.

"When I come back it won't be anything like the way I'm leaving."

Then he moved closer to perhaps kiss just her cheek, to seal those words, but she clasped him with both hands and kissed him on the lips. It was a first kiss, in front of her uncle and godmother, with a dozen soldiers and workmen looking on silently and sheepishly. But it was a real kiss and one that he'd waited his whole life for, in case it was the last one.

No one knew but him that this was what he'd wished for under Kepler's Arch.

Chapter Ten

Reckoning

Terra saw to it that Borealis would never be a problem again and without even disrupting for a beat the never-ending shipments of helium-3 that headed to all parts. Terra never meant to destroy her prideful rival; that would have been to devalue their very prize. Instead, Borealis was just decapitated and rendered at a stroke the most precious jewel in the Terran Ring's crown.

The Terran attack fleet had scanned oddly from the start. It was comprised of relatively few warships and an unreasoned number of freighters—*empty* cargo ships. The anomaly was explained by the 12,657 names listed on the warrants served. Every public official, engineer, doctor, scientist, and business executive on Borealis was under arrest and sooner or later shuttled to waiting transports in lunar orbit. Terran colonists, selected in advance from an index of the most able applicants, awaited their opportunity to flood in to take their places. With stunning rapidity, Borealis was changed overnight almost, with an unrelenting and quick-stepped military precision. Even the age-old proverbs from ancient Earth knew that in times of war the law is helpless and mute, and nothing had changed. There was only silence now about lunar partition, helium-3 rights, and war or peace in the Asteroid Belt, and anywhere else.

There had never been a set piece battle between large fleets in space—until the recent unexplained encounter, which was no battle at all, only a massacre. Strategists who had prepared to see their tactics validated now realized the game had changed so quickly. Their visions for how victory was to be wrested between fleets of indestructible warships would never be tested. It was as if they had drawn up plans for warfare between dirigibles when suddenly a biplane appeared on the horizon.

Tacticians had imagined dozens of warships engaged in hundreds of overlapping dogfights within an enormous three-dimensional battlefield. The goal would be to force an opposing warship into the destructive radius of an exploding tactical nuke, while keeping one's own vessels outside these danger zones. Many factors would affect the outcome of this type of war of attrition: speed and angle of attack, numbers and disposition of forces in the field, and of course, the quantity of nuclear firepower stored on board in magazines. Just as important would be the morale and toughness of the combatants; war games showed that a grinding slug fest was the likely scenario. Serious concussion blasts from nuclear explosions would crack the molyserilium coating on wounded vessels and those vulnerable spots would show up on enemy scanners, drawing laser fire from any opponent with a clear line of sight. Unprotected sections of stricken ships would have to be jettisoned, and quickly. The new molyserilium exteriors, laid bare by the loss of the destroyed compartments, would now be an integral part of damaged vessels' laser reflector—hopefully. A warship could go on fighting, theoretically, for as long as its crew could stand being pummeled with non-stop g forces, while slowly losing parts of itself and squads of its crew, until a vital section were lost and every crewman on board was killed. The greatest advantage a manned warship had was due to the old-fashioned, hard to beat human capacity for patching and fixing on the fly. Fire ships and unmanned decoys were also part of the fleet, adding a further layer of complexity to the grueling match. Military scientists on both sides imagined a fight like that in store for the Terran and Borelian fleets closing on each other.

The great contest ended with even less than a whimper though, because it never took place at all. Borealis had other matters with which to contend now, and capturing and bringing home the Object fell from the highest order of the most crucial undertaking of the state, to below worth mentioning directly as the order to disperse was issued. For there was no base to which to bring "home" the prize. Borealis, within hours, was to be converted into a puppet-state of the Terran Ring, a Vichy, only providing helium-3 to the conquerors instead of wine.

Standing and fighting now had very much the look of cavalry charging tanks. It had been done in history, but not too well, not lately. The Borelian fleet followed the last order of the Council, abandoning the Object to the victorious Terrans, fleeing toward the Outer, their morale matching their situation.

One of the few of the 12,657 indicted by Terra yet not in custody on the Ring was—Clinton Rittener. There *are* those who say that the canister he rode off the Moon only escaped being instantly vaporized by the circling Terran fleet because they had orders not to fire. This hard-bitten, pessimistic scenario has Rittener far from a reformed mercenary trying to make amends for his life with a lasting peace, and rather as an agent of Terra after all, superbly ensconced now within whatever remained of the Borelian resistance. In their suspicious, world-weary view, Terra permitted him to be sent straight into the bosom of the last remaining cadre of armed resistance—the Borelian fleet. The truth, though, was quite a bit different from this spine-tingling, clandestine, double-agency. Like most truths compared to speculation, it was patently prosaic.

No one had ever taken a suicidal ride off the Moon inside a helium-3 canister. Strapped in, cushioned with foam, and injected with a concoction of pharmacons that played dangerous games with internal organs and blood vessels, Rittener, even as the sedatives took effect just before launch, didn't hold much hope himself.

"This doesn't have a chance of actually working, does it?" Rittener groggily asked the chief engineer before the hatch was slid shut and locked.

"Just lay back and keep your fingers crossed," the chief answered, stowing the barest of essential supplies and tugging on the belts and straps. He added with a false bravado, "We've got a few tricks up our sleeves to get Emma to go a little easier on you." Since it had never been attempted it was certainly true, "We've never lost anyone yet."

The cartridge would have scanned something like a normal helium-3 canister, being mostly gas; and there was no weaponry, machinery or complicated circuitry within. It was headed away from the fleet, in the direction of Mars.

And, unbeknownst to conspiracy theorists, there *was* an order to refrain from firing on outgoing helium-3 canisters. The Terran Ring was eager to show the entire Solar System that there was nothing terrible transpiring in this little fuss between themselves and Borealis. All was going to be well, better even, with Terra now firmly at the helm. Helium-3 was on its way, like it always was. So thanks to Terran politics, and the fog of combat, by hook or by crook, Clinton Rittener made it off the Moon, eclipsing escape velocity, and coasting toward the emptiness of black space.

Aside from the few refugees on the few warships of a state that existed no more, everyone with any sense in the Solar System was cowed by this tremendous upturn in the fortunes of the Terran Ring. The people of Earth, Mars, the Asteroid Belt and the Jovian Moons, and as far out as Titan, had all only just been stunned with the news of the Object's existence. Now they found that Borealis had been extinguished over it, by the use of weapons beyond the ken of current military technology, perhaps it quite realistically and frighteningly seemed now, developed by the use of super advanced extraterrestrial sources to which Terra had access. If everything was moving too fast, it wasn't moving too quickly for diplomats everywhere to quickly adopt the same position: the surrender was immediate and total. No one lifted a finger or said a word in Borealis' defense, each state outdoing the other in its slavish pronouncements of allegiance to Terra. A truly new age had dawned and anyone could see that it was to be the Terran Ring that would be the protagonist in the chronicle to be written.

It was an Eastern Alliance ship, *Kasuga*, under Captain Kanda Minoru, who picked him up. It was safer for fleeing Borelian warships to keep their distance, so the last gambit of having an allied vessel link up with Rittener seemed more prudent. Minoru, who knew Rittener personally, having served with him in Asia, probably would have been faithful to his erstwhile comrade, as would have been the Eastern Alliance. Like most bellicose states on Earth, not knowing when to quit, and always keeping the dream alive of somehow, some way getting a blow in on Terra, their real policy hadn't changed—even now. The proof of that is that Minoru didn't deliver the body to Terran authorities, or even apprise them of his demise. Instead he consigned the body to burial in space, with full military honors, befitting a fallen commander in the Borelian Service.

Rittener, like so many of his generation, like so many children of groaning Earth in his age—starved, beaten, dispossessed, impoverished—didn't leave a scrap of physical evidence behind of his having even existed. Ultimately, he was a failure, like everyone on Earth during this sad, brutal, life-snuffing era. He'd failed actually in the end, at everything he did, while making it appear from time to time that his stunning strings of seeming successes were actually going somewhere. There is one thing though that he accomplished that will last for an eternity. In a way, he'd placed into perpetuity a very poignant monument to Earth, one that should remain circling Sol long, long after the Terran Ring itself ceased to be. He carried with him into his final orbit, forever circling the Sun in the dead, somber space between Earth and Mars, a token of a turn mankind should have made at the beginning of the killing centuries before it was too late. His far removed ancestor and some unknown

183

British Tommie had known that, and here was the proof on his dead finger, floating tens of millions of miles above the senseless battlefields of the Western Front—a red salmon, leaping happily over three blue waves—the insignia of the Second Corps, but really the symbol of mankind's age-old, unrequited dream of...peace.

Cosmologists know that humanity and Earth have both ridden quite an amazing lucky streak. A bit closer or further away from the Sun and the blue paradise planet would be frozen or broiled. But for her weighty satellite, Moon, to steady her axis, and Earth's roiling, turbid, molten core to generate her radiation blocking magnetic shield, the planet would have remained a barren and lonely place. At every step of a billions year long saga, whenever the die were cast, with survival or death in the balance, Earth's life force overcame all no matter how long the odds. No lucky streak lasts forever though.

It was bad luck, indeed, that the Object detonated precisely when it did, when Earth's eastern hemisphere had wheeled under the section of the Terran Ring in which it was docked and quarantined. The last time an explosion this violent and strong occurred, in these environs of the Solar System, was four billion years ago when the proto-Earth collided with Mars-sized Theia to create the Moon. The blast instantly vaporized half of Terra, the entire semicircular section of the Ring, ninety degrees in both directions from the epicenter of the detonation. The force of the explosion tore through the Terran Ring like a sledgehammer through a cloud, and reached down to the surface of the planet to boil off the top layers of the oceans below, and to sterilize Europe, Africa and Asia. The Old World disappeared—just like that.

On the other side of the Ring, the sections above Earth's western hemisphere, death came just a few heartbeats later. For the Terran Ring was no longer a "ring"; half of it had been erased. What remained was a shattered, fracturing, boomerang-shaped reservoir of potential energy that was now going horrifically, unbelievably, wildly—kinetic. It wobbled awkwardly, surreally, spinning once around the globe, playing out its inertia, before plunging to Earth in a ghastly dive, a fall so terrifying and unthinkable that the sound alone shattered the eardrums of most of the people still alive on Earth.

The sky—actually—*was* falling.

It was falling, and coming down on South America. Country-sized pieces of the Ring crashed to the ground at what had once been Ecuador, Peru, Venezuela, Colombia and Brazil. These places, along with almost all of Amazonia, which burned for months, disappeared as identifiable locales, their former identities pounded beyond recognition as trillions of tons of steel slammed into them at terminal velocity.

The rest of what remained of the Ring splashed into the Pacific and Atlantic Oceans, pieces many hundreds of miles long, some thousands of miles in length, raising tsunamis of unfathomable height, extent and power. Coastlines around the planet were drowned. Central America was overtopped; all the land from Panama to Mexico completely submerged as immeasurable quantities of water sloshed out of the oceanic basins and then receded again.

185

Humanity had taken a savage punch, meant to be a killing blow. It didn't exterminate the human race, however, but it did send Earth stumbling backwards several centuries. And, of course, the Terran Ring, with its five billion inhabitants was just—gone. When those survivors still alive on Earth, mostly in the heartland of North America which had been spared, summoned the temerity to cautiously leave their homes and gaze up, a dumbfounded look was written across their faces. That same expression could be seen for many, many years whenever people looked up toward the equatorial skies, still not really sure that such an eternal feature in the heavens was actually, in fact—just gone.

The Terran Ring *was* gone, and with it went its age. Everything changed.

Borealis survived, actually was saved by the "Event," as it was called. Yes, at first there was a period of unrestrained rioting and disorder, as mobs hunted down and exterminated any of the unfortunate Terran overlords who had barely arrived to administer the newly acquired province. These ill-fated taskmasters now couldn't care less about helium-3 or any of the other great questions that had animated them yesterday. Their only concern now was how to manage to go on breathing hour by hour. When the bloodlust abated and cooler heads prevailed, Borealis realized how important these former conquerors were. The pool of scientists, engineers, doctors, administrators and others necessary to efficiently run a society had been dangerously thinned, with billions of them just recently having been evaporated. Borealis' entire intelligencia, sadly, had been among them, incarcerated on the Ring—Nerissa, too. They also realized

186

that the Terran Ring's own storm trooper tactics, which had wrested the Object from Borealis' grasp, was ironically the very means by which the city had been saved, while the Ring destroyed. A marriage of convenience was hastily arranged and the last several thousand Terrans alive were assimilated into Borelian society.

That society was irrevocably sent down a different path. The price of helium-3 plummeted as fast as the Ring had fallen. Simply put, Borealis' customers were all dead. There was still a demand for it in the Outer and piddling amounts were sent to clients on Earth. The consignments for Earth, though, in a morbid yet telling way, were designated "American." Mother Earth, laid so low, having been downgraded from a world to just a continent, now almost lost her very name, the Borelians giving that catch-all moniker to anyone living on the planet below, including the few Australians, Argentines, and Chileans left with whom they also did business. But business was bad, and getting worse all the time.

The Event produced the profoundest effects in the Outer though, its aftermath forging the path of the course history was to follow. No matter the dreadful result, Mars, Titan, the Jovian colonies and all the rest had seen everything unfold with their own eyes. The Object *did* move at just a fraction below light speed, must have combined astounding amounts of anti-matter—measured in the untold *tons*—to combine with matter to effect such an explosion, and gave tantalizing clues as it streaked toward Earth that it certainly *wasn't* propelled by helium-3 but by quite a different energy source. Harnessing the power of vacuum fluctuations had been a dream with roots stretching as far back as the 20th Century. It now became a real goal. The bizarre irony of the

Event was that, in destroying Earth, it was the single greatest impetus transforming humanity into the anchorless, space faring people that they became. If it had been the purpose of the Object to exterminate mankind, the result of the attack not only failed to snuff out completely the cradle of human civilization, but strengthened its reign tenfold, a hundred fold, by sending its tentative shoots out in every direction toward the stars. Titan was the first to construct an actual, working quantum ramjet. The colonies on the Jovian System followed up this astonishing achievement by mining anti-matter, and appreciable quantities of it, from—well, from nothing. The void itself—endless, ubiquitous, eternal—became the new larder to satisfy man's hunger for energy. This pantry could never run out.

Borealis, just a century later, was nothing more than a curiosity, with visitors taking in the place for the history, but wondering what people actually *did* here, besides play their role in a city that was more museum than anything else. The great mansions were still there, but like grand saloons in ghost towns, even children could tell something was missing that used to be here. Parents explained things by taking their youngsters on excursions outside the city. The Field was one of the most visited tourist attractions in the Solar System so at least the Moon was left looking handsome and well-groomed. The harvesters had raked the lunar surface neatly—great, continental sized sections of the Moon—squeezing Luna dry of helium-3, and in their wake leaving the greatest Japanese rock garden in the universe.

"What was helium-3, Mom? Did they burn it?" The young would ask. Parents realized that it was easy for their children to confuse it with the one before. "No, son, it was petroleum they burned."

As for Earth, well, for the first time in centuries it had peace. Cynics explained the phenomenon by pointing out that there were too few able-bodied men left on Earth to field an army. The Event, as mind-numbingly awful as it was, still was but the last and most brutal in a series of seemingly unending blows of death and destruction that had rained on Earth. It was, though, the tipping point. Whether mankind was to take this new opportunity to begin again properly, by disavowing violence finally and forever, by husbanding its resources suitably, by becoming astute stewards finally of the planet to which they'd fallen heir—all of this slowly, strangely, inexorably lost its power to interest even. Humanity, as if finally falling out of love with a dysfunctional paramour, was starting to look the other way: outward.

It didn't happen in a great rush, like so many for gold, oil, and land. It was more like spores on a soft but steady breeze rustling through a meadow on a fine day. The center of gravity of civilization had moved away from the Sun, its warmth and power finally, after so many eons, having lost the allure to hold its children spellbound any longer. And those on the far edges, slowly, inevitably, cautiously, simply let go.

Chapter Eleven

Red Blood

The ten year-old had been squirming in his chair through the whole story. Fidgeting, that is, up to the last part when the Terran Ring and Earth were destroyed. This chapter of the saga always got his attention, no matter how many times he had to listen to his parents tell it. This was also a good place for him to attempt to deflect attention away from the fact that he was being reprimanded. He diverted it by asking the question that had been posed by every ten year-old who ever heard the old, old epic tale.

"Who built the Object, Dad? Who built it, and why did they do that?"

The boy's father could have been called the salt of the Earth, even though that locale was ten and a half light years away. He was a farmer, the elected foreman of one of the agricultural consortiums that produced prodigious quantities of the two oldest staples of the old mother planet, bread and wine, but enough of it to fill the pantries and cellars of every living soul in the Epsilon Eridani system. It was a good life out here and that could be seen in husband, wife and son. They were perfect specimens, reflecting the healthful, life-giving bounty of the planet their great-grandparents had chosen for them as home. Things simply sprang to life on

Arcadia, the word for "paradise" in Greek. It was complained, and not without excuse, that the only reason it wasn't christened Eden was due to the fact that the name was already taken—by the moon orbiting the first planet around Barnard's Star. The truth was, though, that this second planet from Epsilon Eridani, with its amethyst sky, orange sun, and pale pink colored clouds was more paradisiacal than that moon in the Barnardian system, or any other known planet.

Arcadia's benevolence surpassed even that of Earth's—possessing all the life-nurturing qualities of the mother planet with none of her flaws. There were no deserts, tundra, or badlands on Arcadia, only a lush carpet of fruit-giving vegetation from equator to poles. Science marveled at the amazing jackpot that Arcadia was, imagining that Earth had been about as far as one could hope to push the odds in favor of a habitable abode for life transformed out of the chaos of the cosmos. Earth wasn't though, nor Eden; Arcadia was the reigning champion of freakishly lucky planets.

Though sizably smaller than Earth, Arcadia was so much denser that the gravity was only slightly weaker. A thick atmosphere, rich in oxygen, carbon dioxide and nitrogen securely enveloped the smaller, condensed sphere. This world also was nearer to Epsilon Eridani than Earth was to Sol but that too was in perfect harmony. The planet huddled just near enough to the lesser, cooler orange star for its red-shifted light to bathe Arcadia's vegetation in the most optimally tuned spectrum of light for growth and warmth. All the countervailing forces were ideally balanced on Arcadia as if perfectly tuned by some universal deity amusing himself with a cosmic chemistry set. Temperature, pressure, atmospheric composition, the intensity and wavelength of the sunlight, the perfectly synchronized cycles of water, nitrogen and carbon—all those parameters and a thousand others had been adroitly calibrated in such a way as to put out the most famous welcome sign for life in the known Milky Way.   But the greatest long shot that had come in for Arcadia was her absolutely unique celestial mechanics. So far this was the only planet ever discovered that revolved and spun in just the way Arcadia did.

Revolving around Epsilon Eridani and spinning on her axis, there were years and days, like on any planet. Here, though, there was only one season, stuck just where spring turns into summer. Most cosmologists believed that some collision in Arcadia's past struck the planet an extremely unlikely, but just as lucky a blow. The celestial missile would have clipped the planet with the most extreme English, glancing one of her poles at just exactly zero degrees, causing Arcadia to flip end over end, pole over pole, while she rotated in front of and revolved around Epsilon Eridani. Some rare dynamic, in any event, was the cause of the current slow, lethargic, blessed cartwheel Arcadia turned while gliding in orbit around her star. The gentle, favored roll that gave each latitudinal swath of Arcadia its equal moments at the equator, both poles, and at every parallel between was unknown anywhere else in existence. It was as if colonists had come upon Arcadia on the very night of her prom, and captivated by the most beautiful belle around any star seen anywhere, immediately promised themselves to this virginal territory.

Arcadia—pristine, untouched, fertile, gorgeous—might be compared to a virgin, but a unique virgin, one constantly pregnant. It was said things sprouted on Arcadia just by *thinking* about growing them, and that was only a slight exaggeration. Rain came every night, falling gently in a baby-light mist all night, everywhere—but storms were unknown. Since it was springtime everywhere every day on Arcadia, and with the rich, plentiful carbon dioxide for plants and the super abundance of oxygen for its creatures, this planet of eternal summer was the scene of an explosion of life of all kinds.

The concept of widespread death and destruction were only alive in the age-old stories and epics from Earth and even though the boy had asked the question before, this time, now a bit older, his tone and expression told the father that a more adult answer now was required.

"No one knows who built it, son. Nor how old it was, nor even if it was meant specifically for humanity. It may simply have been patrolling space to wipe out in advance any up and coming civilization that might be a potential rival to them, whoever they were—or are. No one knows."

He scrutinized his child's face for acknowledgement of understanding. The boy was certainly thinking it all over.

"Or maybe even," the father went on, "it might have been constructed on Earth, by humans, but from a very, very distant past age."

His wife didn't like that at all, and let him know by rolling her eyes to make sure her husband perceived her discomfiture.

"I saw something from one of the Earth channels on that!" The boy quickly answered happily. Here was another sidebar he seemed quite willing to explore with his parents. The mother most certainly had an opinion on that too. She picked up her son's confiscated slingshot and put it his face.

"Well, but we certainly know who built *this*, don't we?" She was shaking her head and frowning. "Is that where you learned how to make this, from an Earth channel?" The wrinkled forehead and raised eyebrows of his mother reminded him that this also was a bone of contention: Earth content.

The most important thing still exchanged with the old world was information and news, even though the reports were ten and a half years old. The familial bond between Mother Earth and Arcadia was still strong though. The Epsilon Eridani system and Earth stayed in daily, hourly, minute to minute contact with each other, only the conversation was a little strained, hampered by a decade long light lag. And nothing, not even sixty three trillion miles, could stamp out completely the age-old, atavistic need to trade. There *were* the rarest, most exotic goods still bartered back and forth over the mind-numbing distances of interstellar space, even if the bills of lading showed a decade or more between departure and arrival. This sort of commerce was left to syndicates of long-term investors who, weathering the risk and the delay, appropriately reaped impossible profits trading between stars. Wine from Arcadia was shipped to its stellar neighbors, and to a far, far lesser extent, as an exotic curiosity, its wheat too. Both were exorbitantly expensive, beyond almost anyone's wallet or purse. No church on Earth could afford to have communion of such distinct, top-drawer ingredients consecrated. For the gourmet to whom price meant nothing though, goods baked with plump, maltose-rich Arcadian wheat were the most delicious of any that had been tasted since the first loaf came out of the brick ovens of pharaonic Egypt. And, for

Arcadian wines, words were also useless. It was the opinion of many connoisseurs that it was best, for those who had to import it, to never let it pass one's lips, lest either a lifetime of appreciation for other quite pedigreed vintages be irrevocably lost, or one's finances ruined in crippling arbitrage.

The most obvious hallmark that the interstellar business wasn't like any other pursuit, was that relativistic effects required that time-dilation clauses be written into contracts. Arcadian wine, for example, didn't age normally in transit, and just-pressed product shipped straight off the vine to Earth was only half as expensive as properly aged vintages. There was no cheating the aging paradox, and Einstein's equations were obeyed by everyone, and everything— including beverages. Wine, whiskey, cheese and other goods that matured didn't gain much ground traveling at close to the speed of light for most of the journey between stellar systems. And neither did the voyagers that accompanied the merchandise, giving birth to that strangest class of people who had ever lived. Stellar travelers, who traded away a few years to jump forward a dozen hence, were said to be vaguely, perceptibly "out of sync." There was something slightly ill-omened about those with the inclination to spend two or three years, according to *their* clocks, to arrive at a place a dozen light-years away, under a Sun of a different color, a decade in the future. Enough of it, and one could surely go "star crossed."

There were many new things to get used to, or endure at least, living out in the stars a dozen light years in all directions from Earth. Not something that gained immediate attention, but seen by almost everyone after a while, was a certain malaise out here, barely tangible, but a recognized melancholy born of the intense distances and acute solitude. Providing a salve for the feeling of bleak desolation that rubbed at people's souls; this was Arcadia's real claim to fame, not her wine nor her pastries. Where pacifism and nonaggression had guided the politics and culture of all the extra-solar worlds, on Arcadia it became a rigorous philosophy, and then a religion. Tibet, Mecca, the Vatican, and the Holy Land were all gone as fonts which soothed the collective consciousness of humanity—but there was Arcadia. Her greatest export, like classical Athens almost four millennia before, swept through the hard-won area of the spiral arm of the galaxy where mankind had laid down roots: words and ideas.

"Do you understand why your father and I are so disappointed in your behavior?" She asked her son. The boy lowered his eyes. He knew that tone and realized that no answer was going to do. Experience taught him that silence was best now. She wouldn't have it though.

"Answer me," she snapped.

"They were just sludgeskimmers." The boy knew his mother couldn't appreciate how much fun it was to target them with his slingshot. They actually exploded a lot of the time if they were hit properly, puncturing bladders that fizzled like fireworks in the oxygen-rich air. They were such bizarre creatures, half insect, half bird, part dragonfly, part firefly, mostly alien hummingbird.

"They were just sludgeskimmers. Please, mother…" The boy just blurted it out; he couldn't hide his exasperation. Nor, unfortunately, could his mother.

"You're going to have some time to think of a better answer for me, young man," she promised threateningly.

And to leave no doubt about the menace, she let have at her son, sternly lecturing him, bringing tears to his eyes.

"Just sludgeskippers? That's your answer?" She railed at him. All sins, every piece of ugliness that ever existed or ever would, all the dark, evil, debilitating defeats and failures of mankind, in every age, all stemmed from the same primal, spiteful poison: violence. Brute force hid the true shortcomings of laziness and stagnation, since it was easier for the dull and sluggish to steal what they thought they required than to create it. Covetousness and prideful envy, theft, murder and finally warfare and annihilation—these and other weaknesses, vices, and crimes were nothing but the exposed gangrene of violence, let loose on the body of humankind, who still after all this time, had not been totally inoculated against it.

Beautiful, bountiful Arcadia held the shining beacon pointing to a different vision, just as steadfastly lighting the way for those who lost sight of the true task of mankind—to fill the Milky Way with life. If in past epochs even sages had pondered without answer what the meaning of existence was, that great enigma had been solved for the fortunate generation alive now, and those to come. Mother Earth, a single blue-green speck in the dead, silent void, had produced a progeny of demigods with the power and animus to convert the amorphous chaos of the galaxy into a vibrant, death-defying reflection of themselves—and their mother. That was the task at hand and only internecine conflict, only fratricidal violence and war could stop them now. There *were* true perils in the infinite universe against which humanity must forever remain united, and such a future required a sophisticated race that could not be lackadaisical toward death, who would detest violence as sport. Man's long, fitful, appalling journey through darkness was finally coming to an end, the religion born on Arcadia said, and that gloom should never be allowed to return. This view, this powerful idea, was spreading.

She knew a child of ten couldn't understand most of this. But that was no reason for her, a good Arcadian, a decent woman, a proud mother, to risk allowing her own son to be tainted with the worst venom she could imagine. The idea that the boy should have found pleasure in killing something filled her with a terrifyingly powerful disgust. She was going to extirpate this failing in her son, and do it completely, immediately, remorselessly.

"Didn't you learn anything at all from the story your father just told you? Do you understand how Borealis' and Terra's and Earth's silly addiction to slingshots and other weapons left them vulnerable to the greatest danger? You don't grasp that?" She didn't wait for a response, but just pointed imperiously in the direction of his room.

"One whole period. You're on restriction for a period." She let the term of the sentence sink in, and then fired the second salvo. "And we'll have to see about Earth content. Your father and I are going to do some thinking about what sort of things have been influencing you. We'll talk about this some more, later." She pointed toward his room. "Restriction, starting now."

His father came in later that evening to say goodnight. The boy had already turned in for bed, and was laying with his head buried in his pillow, pouting. As soon as he realized it was just his father, and that his dad had an almost conciliatory smile on his face, he perked up.

"You know, everything your mother said, well, she's right about all that." He tousled his son's hair. "I'm counting on you to take your medicine like a man. You're not going to let me down, are you?"

The boy was shaking his head in agreement with his father. "Good, then we can put this behind us for tonight and get some sleep." His father gave him a last roughly affectionate tweak and pulled the covers up tight under his chin. For a moment the boy thought his father was going to give him a kiss, staring down at him like that, but it was because he had something to share with his son.

"The truth is that I was ten years old once myself. And, as long as you don't mention this to your mother, I've popped a few sludgeskimmers in my day, too." His father winked at him. "So don't feel too badly about it, alright?" The boy nodded and father and son said goodnight.

On his way out of the room he was stopped by his son's question. "Can I ask you something, Dad?"

The boy was up on elbow, recovered from the tongue-lashing his mother had given him, the inquisitive, impish look back in his eyes.

"Is it possible that Clinton Rittener didn't die blasting off from the Moon like that?" His father almost chuckled to himself, wondering on which channel he might have heard that.

"Some say, maybe," the boy went on, "that he barely made it, and went on searching for the aliens who attacked Earth. Could that be true, Dad?"

As he dimmed the light he couldn't think of any good reason why his son shouldn't have at least one hero, like any other boy.

"I suppose that might be true. It happened a long, long time ago and there's no telling for sure about those kinds of things. Goodnight, Son." Now the farmer *did* chuckle to himself as he left his son's bedroom, imagining the boy fantasizing about heroes chasing down and punishing the dastardly alien beings who'd brutalized Earth in ages past.

The boy's thoughts though had turned away from childish whimsies and toward forbidden plans as he drifted off to sleep. Another slingshot, his favorite, was safely ensconced in the makeshift fort in which he and his companions played. The boy legionnaires had toiled diligently on their secret citadel, constructed of twisted and woven briars, vines and branches, and camouflaged perfectly within the thicket of which it was made. He didn't like disobeying his mother but the thrill he experienced tramping about in the wilds with his comrades appealed too strongly to him to ignore so easily. And, popping sludgeskimmers was the most fun a boy could have on Arcadia. He wasn't about to give that up either, no matter how many boring lectures his mother made him sit and swallow. He would be more careful; he'd have to be. Because nothing could change the fact that he was happiest when testing his strength and agility in the bush, pitting his skills against the creatures that flew in and out of his slingshot's sight, and doing it all in competition with his friends who loved it too.

He may have lived tens of trillions of miles and thousands of years away from uncountable boys on Earth who had woken up in the morning and gone to bed at night thinking of their next adventure in the open air. But that same red

201

blood ran through his veins, too. He cared more for jumping, wrestling, stalking, and running than he did for any brave new world his mother or any other mother could imagine.

The fact was that he couldn't help but give in to the scrappy, impetuous virility of his gender, a force that was coded into every chromosome in his body, and which gave him a feeling that seemed as natural and fitting as breathing. He not only surrendered to it but reveled in it, like boys have always done, everywhere, before him in the past.

And—like boys always will.